Kick

The Perdition Series – Book One

D1521742

CD REISS

kick

CHAPTER 1

My ankles were shackled. The chain between them clicked when I rolled over, and the steel bit my anklebones when I rested my feet together.

My brain chemistry had been set for arousal at the touch of hard metal edges on my skin, and even though I felt a growing swirl of lust when I pressed my legs together, I was preoccupied. Deacon hadn't put the leg irons on me, nor had I squeezed them tighter than I should, just to feel them holding me while he played me like a musician at an instrument.

I didn't know what had happened.

The last thing I remembered was rain.

No. The last thing I remembered was being in scene with Deacon and entering subspace, outside of myself, where pleasure and pain merged.

No.

Nuzzling Snowcone as he huffed and clopped his hoof on the stable floor, I held his bit. I thought, *he's slow, it's over, he's slow, he's old, it's over, he won't take the bit, he's slow.* My thoughts repeated as if they were stuck.

The last thing I remembered was hanging from the ceiling, listening to rain on the windows. It never rained in Los Angeles—unless it did, and then it rained like a holy hail of fuck yous.

The last thing I remembered was wet thighs. Feeling so sore I couldn't sit. Thinking about fucking. Finding someone to fuck.

There was so much fucking.

The last thing I remembered was snorting a line of flake off Amanda's tits.

And then?

Nothing.

Anxiety sat in my chest like a kinetic weight, but I wasn't scared. I knew I wasn't thinking right, that I was little more than a jumble of emotions and half sentences. I thought in colors, and saw in bursts of silence. The aggressive white light above illuminated the angles of the corners. The tight space and soft white walls were the product of some kind of regulating entity. Was I in prison? A hospital? Was I even in the United States? When would Deacon come for me?

Soon.

He'd come soon, and everything would be in control again.

Until then, I'd submit to the fog of my half-formed thoughts and nothing would go wrong.

kick.

***

"Do you know where you are?"

His voice was so gentle in powder blues and jazzy notes, but he was a stranger. I'd never heard a voice like that—thick and soft as heavy cream, a satin sheet on a bed of sand. I opened my eyes to bright white fog and a charcoal blur that must have been attached to the voice. Not a cop. Not a lawyer. Not an ER doc.

"No," I croaked.

"I'm going to ask you some questions. All right?"

I nodded. I didn't realize how quiet it was until the noise of the sheet rubbing against my ear sounded like an electric guitar amp set to eleven.

"Can you tell me your name?"

It wasn't loud, that voice. Like Deacon's, it had its own kind of authority, but unlike my master's, it was gentle.

I cleared the frog from my throat. "Fiona."

"Hi, Fiona. My name is Doctor Chapman. But you can call me Elliot."

My eyes cleared a little. The charcoal smear turned into a beige oval with two green-grey dots for eyes and non-committally colored hair. His skin wrinkled around the eyes, but his mouth was young. He was either in his late twenties, or forty-ish, like Deacon. Or maybe somewhere in between.

"Good," he said, crouching to meet my gaze. "How old are you?"

"Twenty-three."

"Where do you live?"

That was a hard question, with its own complexity.

"The first thing that comes to mind," the doctor said.

"Number three, Maundy Street."

He nodded, so my answer must have been satisfactory. "Get cleaned up, get something to eat, then we can talk."

I nodded, and the noise in my ear was less shocking. He stood and went for the white door with the little window at eye level.

"Where am I?" I asked.

"Westonwood Acres."

***

They fed me in my room from a metal tray. I didn't eat much. I was shown to a small bathroom, where I was expected to clean up and change out of one light blue jumpsuit into another. I had never been squeamish about germs or ickiness, but in the soft cotton of my mind, something seemed inherently wrong with the space, the room, the clothes.

Deacon would find me. He was probably in some office right now, demanding my release from the mental ward. He had a way of sniffing me out, even when I snuck away, as if he and I were connected by a vibrating fiber. No matter how far I went, no matter how fast, he knew. If there was anyone in the world I could count on, it was him. He was coming. All I had to do was behave long enough for him to arrive.

Just thinking of him, the bones of his wrist, the tendons tight on his forearms when he gripped my body, his growl—*mine mine mine*—sent a wave of pleasure between my legs.

I knew who I was. I was a celebrity without talent. I was an heiress. I was a whore. I was a party waiting to happen. I was an addict. I was his, and in that last definition—that I was owned by Deacon I knew my place in the chaos.

Sitting on the edge of my bed, the headache came like slowly tightening wrenches clamped to my temples and the back of my neck. As the pain bloomed, my mind cleared. Though I couldn't remember shit any better than before, I gained the good sense to worry about it. I gained details. Cast-iron grates on the windows in a decorative pattern. No doorknob. Walls of suede microfiber. Cork floors. Soft wood bed with Egyptian cotton sheets.

There were people around me, but I felt more than saw them. Intuited their presence. How long had I been walking through plasma? Where was the other side?

The last thing I remembered… What was the last thing I remembered? It was Deacon in the kitchen of number three, sweatpants and no shirt, with his arms out. He was saying something. Pleading. He was telling me I had to kick. Kick? What did that mean? And was it the kitchen or the stables? Whatever space he was in was plagued by his raw pain. He was mad and resigned at the same time, two things I'd never seen from him.

Was that the last thing I remembered? Whatever it was must have landed me here.

There had been a dream with red and blue lights.

There had been a party, possibly before the lights, maybe after. I was on my hands and knees. I was high, so high, flooded with endorphins and knocking around subspace. My ache was dulled to pleasure, and I wanted something desperately.

I couldn't put it all together. Maybe I'd gone just a little heavy on the flake. Deacon would be pissed. I'd apologize. We'd do a knotting, and I'd get better.

The last thing… Deacon had gone away. He'd put his face in my neck, and I was surrounded by peppermint and sandalwood. He'd gotten in the limo, and I watched it glide down the hill and past the gate of the private road, splashing in the rushing water of the drainage dip. Maundy Street. Left turn past Debbie and Martin's place, and away.

Christmas. He said he'd be back for Christmas.

The house had seemed big, and I'd thought about spending the week at home in Bel-Air. Avoid Debbie. Avoid Martin. Their eyes and their temptations pressed against me. I could handle it. I could handle anything. I was strong.

Was that decision even worth remembering? What was the last thing that had *happened*?

I only remembered stuff from long ago. A knotting, the last one, my favorite. Deacon had laced me to hooks in the ceiling with patterns of knotted rope, turning my body into a work of art. I was upside down, naked, falling from the sky, and he crouched on the floor, caressing my head and shoulders. I always felt at peace when he knotted me, but that time, when he became part of the work, my very identity and all the anxiety that came with it melted away.

Something about a horse, but I must have been dreaming. I hadn't touched a horse in months. Years, maybe.

And the last party. The knots of skin and fluid.

A stinging drip in my nose.

When? Yesterday? Last month? Never?

Now. Here. In Westonwood.

Fuck.

CHAPTER 2

Having eaten a meal in a tiny pale grey room, and walked down wide, pale grey hallway, showered in a white-tiled stall, and gotten into a stainless steel elevator, I found the office jarring. It could have been my headache that grew more potent by the moment, or it could have been the presence of actual colors.

Pale blue curtains drawn against the rain pounding the window. Green lantern. Rich brown wainscoting and desk. Burgundy carpets. I squinted. Even the light from the desk lamp felt intentionally painful.

"Thanks, Bernie," Dr. Chapman said from the corner of the room.

He wore a grey jacket and a sage-green sweater over a white shirt. His voice didn't hurt my head, though when Bernie, the orderly, clicked the door behind him, I felt as if someone had hit my temple with a crowbar.

"Headache?" the doctor asked. I nodded, and he sighed. "For what you pay to be here, you think they'd be on the ball with the analgesics." He slid open a desk drawer and removed a bottle of over-the-counter medicine. "Let me get you some water."

I held out my hand. "Don't need it."

He shook two into my palm. I kept my hand out then spread my fingers wider. He shook out two more. I kept my hand out.

"That's plenty," he said.

I threw them to the back of my throat and swallowed. One caught on the back of my tongue, releasing a wave of sour and bitter, but I took it all.

"Would you like to sit?" He put the bottle back and slid the drawer closed.

"Is that a question? About what I like?"

"It's a suggestion phrased as a question."

A padded leather chair in soft green and worn dark wood sat to my left. I touched the brass studs that kept the leather attached and sat down. Doctor Chapman sat behind the desk, settling his right elbow on the arm of the chair. I didn't know if I was supposed to start with questions about what had happened or why I was there. I didn't know if I should rattle off a list of what I remembered and didn't, or ask just how much trouble I was in, or when Deacon was coming to get me out.

But he saved me the trouble. "Can you tell me the last thing you remember?"

I stiffened. My mouth locked up. I couldn't tell him. "When can I leave?"

"Do you think you should leave?"

"Do you think I should leave?"

"It's more important to know what you think," he said.

"It's more important for *you* to know what I think, and it's more important for me to know what you think. So you first."

He rubbed his upper lip with his middle finger, an odd gesture, then dropped his hand. "You're here for your own protection, at the great expense and effort of your family. I have seventy-two hours to report on whether or not you're a danger to yourself or others."

"How am I a danger?"

"You don't remember?"

"You know I don't."

He put his elbows on the desk and looked right into my eyes. I wanted to know what he saw, other than what everyone saw—a party girl with a permanent smile and spread legs. A balls-to-the-wall princess with an entourage and two wrecked Bentleys in the garage. But more than that, I wanted to know how old he was. He looked so young and so wise at the same time.

"If I tell you why you're here," he said with that gentle voice, "I want to warn you, that you've probably blocked it because it's painful to you."

"Okay." I didn't believe him, but I let him think I'd blocked it. The reason I didn't know was because I'd been drunk or high. Whatever sweet chemicals I'd taken had kept my neurons from connecting.

It must have been bad, and I could never feel guilty about it because I didn't remember it. I'd had a drunk driving accident. I'd given someone bad pills. I'd been gang-fucked and dumped in an alley. I'd killed some random paparazzi. One of the entourage had turned on me. All the things Mom had listed as a fear and Dad had implied with his look.

"You're making me nervous," I whispered even though my headache abated.

"Do you know Deacon Bruce?"

I heard his last name so infrequently, sometimes I forgot he even had one. "Yes."

"Do you remember what he is to you?"

"Yes." I refused to clarify further. He was my safety. My control. The hub on the wheel of my life. Without him, the spokes didn't meet.

And he was coming for me. All I had to do was stall.

"It would help if you told me the last thing you remember."

"I don't remember anything."

"Do you remember going to the Branwyn Stables yesterday?"

"I haven't been to the stables in years." As if the back of my face had a surface all its own, it tingled. A corset tightened around my chest. I was going to cry, and I had no idea why. "I need you to just tell me, Doctor."

"Call me Elliot."

"Fucking tell me right now!"

"Can you stay calm?"

I swallowed a golf ball of cry gunk. "Yes. I'm fine. Yes."

Seconds passed. He watched me as if casually observing a churning barrel of worry.

"I'm fine," I said. "You can tell me. I'll be cool."

"We don't know what happened exactly. There are details missing. Mister Bruce isn't well enough to be interviewed."

I tried to hold myself together, but my fingers gripped the edge of the chair. He saw my knuckles turn white. I knew it, but I had nowhere else for the tension to go.

"Go on," I said.

"There are some things that are known for sure, and some questions. If you remember any portion of what I'm telling you, please stop me."

"Is Deacon okay?"

He cleared his throat and looked away before turning back to me. I realized he didn't want to tell me at all, and that barrel of worry filled up with panic.

"You stabbed him in the chest."

CHAPTER 3

I woke up strapped to the bed with a brain full of fog. Then they took me to a room with a balding doctor and a nurse whose face I couldn't make out through my drug-induced lethargy.

The doctor clucked and groaned as he read things off to the nurse. I could barely sort through what he was saying, and I could barely remember what had happened a few hours ago. Had I attacked someone? The therapist? I'd apologize. He seemed nice. I hoped I didn't hurt him. What had he said to make me freak out? Something about something I did. The reason I was here.

I was in incredible physical shape—I knew that because suspending a woman from the ceiling in rough hemp ropes took hours of work, days of practice, and stamina and strength from both parties. And Deacon, Master Deacon, did not fuck around. I had to get off the flake, reduce the alcohol, and sleep eight hours a day, even if they were when the sun was out. He'd had to watch me sometimes to make sure I ate right, stretched, and stayed off substances, but it was worth it.

Except I was here.

Had Deacon been away?

If he'd been around, I wouldn't have done whatever it was I'd done to land in Westonwood. He'd come and…something. Something was wrong. Something about Deacon. I couldn't find the specifics, but it was something huge and upsetting. My heart beat faster when I tried to think of it. I got impatient with the nurse as she moved my wrist and said a bunch of gibberish as if I wasn't there. She was keeping me from thinking the things I needed to think. Facts lay a layer under the sand, and I was trying to dig them up, but the bitch kept taking my shovel.

The doctor looked at my teeth and poked a molar. A shot of pain cut through me, and I pushed him away so hard he crashed into a tray of torture devices.

Fucking meds. I was going to have to detox again. Once I was curled up in my bed again, I would get the itchy skin, the broken lethargy, the attacks of consciousness that cut into my thoughtless reflections on my sensory space. I'd spent a lot of time trying to get away from my thoughts. Most of my days, actually. I had it down to a science. I never thought about a damn thing.

Or more accurately, I thought plenty and drowned it however I could. When the therapist had told me I'd done something so terrible, such an anathema to me, and I didn't have a substance or an orgasm to drape over the news, I did things without thinking. My determination to be good had gone out the window, and I'd lunged for that lying doctor. I remembered being hauled away screaming, strapped down, and I remembered the injection.

It wasn't until I woke up secured to the bed in a mental ward that I knew what it was like to be distanced from my brain. I could separate the drug thoughts from the real-me thoughts. The drug thoughts were blank and foggy, and the real-me thoughts were black holes where information should have been. Things floated by as if someone was changing the station from a comedy to a thriller to a terror fest to colored bars that went *eeeeeeee*.

I'd stabbed Deacon.

No, it was a lie.

You know it's true.

Not.

Yes.

Not.

You did it.

Never.

I turned my head. Nothing in that room could upset me, because the space was absent of stimuli. The room was still grey, still bathed in light, and in the corner, a silver disk got lost in the vents and alarms dotting the ceiling.

A camera.

If I screamed—and I believed I could—they'd know, and they'd come for me. Or not. I wasn't ready to find out.

I'd been strapped to beds for long periods of time, usually with my legs spread farther than they were now, often with my knees bent. When I was left in that position, it was so I couldn't press my legs closed and give myself an orgasm. By the time Deacon came in, I was wet with anticipation and ready for anything he dished out.

In the hospital, my ankles and wrists were bound so I couldn't hurt myself. I was wet all over again. I tried to close my legs and couldn't. And no one was coming to slap or fuck me. Not even one of Deacon's friends. Not even Debbie. I wasn't strapped down so I could stew in my own lust. I was strapped down because after Elliot had told me I'd stabbed Deacon, my mind had gone white hot.

Fuck.

Even as I got angry at myself over this forgotten thing, I felt the bloat of arousal.

You're swelled, kitten.

Swelled didn't mean horny. That was easy enough. Swelled meant I needed it. Sex. Hot and dirty fucking. Masturbating couldn't stop a swell. Rubbing my cunt on the pillow, vibrators, dildos, eggs, none of them chased away a swell. Only penetration, anywhere, by a warm-blooded man, took care of it. Until that happened, I couldn't function.

It had never been a problem. I took what I wanted, made no commitments, found willing participants wherever, whenever I needed it. I was on three forms of birth control, for fuck's sake. I got tested weekly. I wrapped it up. Past that, my first priority to a swell was getting rid of it, and I was mindless in my pursuit. For Deacon, it became a challenge—to know when I would need it, predict it, and put me in a position where he could withhold penetration. He created the unique torture of being tied in knots, naked, cunt out, ready as he tugged the rope and I begged him to take me.

"I need to finish, kitten. How would it be to have people arrive to a party without the table set?"

He'd hurt me to forestall satisfaction, leaving my ass a deep shade of pink and my little tits sore, putting me on the edge and keeping me there for hours, until I wept.

Had I killed Deacon? My master? Why? How? Oh God, what had I done?

The holes in my mind closed, filled with the thick caulk of sex. I needed it. I needed to feel good. I needed my mind to go blank with pleasure for a second or two, to clear the pain out like a firehose. I could be in for a swell. I needed to feel good. Needed.

"Now!" I cried. "Bathroom!"

Bernie, a big, dark-skinned guy with a kind face, came through the door seconds later. "Hi, Miss Drazen."

He smelled of man, and though he wasn't the best looking guy ever, I was painfully aware of the cock under his blue cotton pants.

"Bernie."

"Yes, ma'am?"

"Do you know anything? About my case?"

"No, ma'am."

He unstrapped me. When his hands touched my wrist, the feeling went right between my legs. I tried to catch his gaze, but his eyes wouldn't meet mine, and I noticed he was trying to avoid touching me. It was as if he knew.

"Thank you." Despite everything, I said it in my softest, most inviting voice.

He let me in the bathroom without another word or touch. When the door snapped shut, I stripped out of the jumpsuit and hitched my leg over the sink. The cold porcelain edge lay hard against my cunt, and I shuddered, clasping my left hand on the faucet, and my right on the edge in front of me.

"Let me come, Sir," I whispered so it wouldn't echo, and I called to mind our first knotting.

***

The twenty-two year old me, the taste of flake a bitter, recent memory, kneels on the wood floor his loft with light pouring in the windows. I am naked but for simple panties. He says that when he ties me naked, he's taking me. We haven't fucked, though our relationship is intensely sexual. He's worth waiting for, this delicious man with his scorching eyes and knowing smirk. I want to obey the rules for him. I feel right when I take care of myself for him.

When Deacon returned from Africa, he sailed, and when he sailed, he knotted mast ropes and women.

He'd been led to what Westerners called shibari. In its ancient form, it was the art of binding prisoners to maximize pain and humiliation. In its modern form, it is the art of patterning rope around a subject for an aesthetic—drawing the lengths around the body to create patterns, to press against erogenous zones, to provide a sexual partner with a compliant, accessible body. The black and white photographs of his work are erotic and sublime, and I knew as soon as he showed me them that I wanted to be part of it.

He puts my hands behind my back and begins. He handles me roughly, moving my body to tie it. There will be no suspension today. Just me, on the floor. It's too soon to risk suspension. I'm not practiced enough. And he won't put anything through my nipple rings until he's sure I can stay still. He's still keeping it simple—teaching me how to hold my hands, checking my reactions, my ability to take instruction, my commitment to safety.

He touches me more than he ever has, and though I'd promised many men I'd be their fuckdoll, for the first time, I actually feel like one. My arms twist behind my back, hands clasping elbows, wrists facing away from the ropes, protected from the pressure. I'm to tell him if anything tingles or feels wrong, but so far, everything is exactly right.

He loops the rope around my ponytail, yanking it so the short rope can be tied to my ankles, and he's done. I'm immobilized, calves to the floor, back arched, forced to look at the hooks in the ceiling from the pressure on the back of my head.

I've never been so aroused. From the tips of my toes to the beating of my heart, my tranquility vibrates with awakening. I feel him standing over me, cutting off the light.

"You doing all right?" he asks.

I open my eyes halfway. He's down to his bare feet and trousers. Shirtless, magnificent Deacon. I can't make words, but my smile answers in the affirmative. He kneels and puts his fingers to my lips. I part them, and he slides them in.

"I'll gag you next time," he says. "The cloth will go around the ropes."

I wet his finger with my tongue. I usually have a ton of dirty talk at my disposal, but I'm so high from this, I can't even speak.

"You'll only be able to grunt, but I'll understand you, kitten. You and I, we're going to speak without speaking."

Lightly, so very lightly, his fingers stroke inside my thigh. I feel my spit drying on them.

"I'm going to tie you and fuck you breathless." He slides my panties aside and runs his finger along the length of my slit. "I've never seen a girl so wet. You really want to fuck."

"I need it." I whisper the only three words I have at the moment.

He gathers the wetness at my tingling opening and moistens me all over, asshole to clit. His pressure is perfect, delicate, gentle. He's not trying to get me to come; he's trying to get me turned on. He slides two fingers in my cunt so slowly, I feel my soul go to heaven.

"You like my fingers?"

I swallow in response. He pulls them out, slowly again, then touches the hood of my clit, shifting it slightly. The effect is hypnotic.

"Look at you," he says, his face close enough to mine that I can smell his peppermint breath. "You're a slave to me right now." He runs his fingers back to my opening, and to my clit, with just the tip, in circles. "Your discomfort is getting crowded out by pleasure. You want to come so bad. This isn't even pleasure. It's the expectation of release. Do you know how long I can keep you going like this? Do you know what I can do to your body? As long as you need that release, I can take you to the breaking point. What wouldn't you do for me?"

He circles a wet finger around my asshole then back to my clit, which feels explosive, engorged, hot to the touch.

"Show me what a kitten you are. Meow for me."

I mewl, wiggling my hips to get a little more pressure on my cunt when he puts his fingers in me. But he and the ropes have complete control.

"Not like that. Don't be saucy. Do it like a real kitten."

"Oh God, just let me—"

He squeezes my clit, and I cry out, because it hurts, and it's just about as close to an orgasm as possible.

He slaps the inside of my thigh. "Easy, girl. The more you demand, the longer I'll keep you on the edge."

I'm sweating, leaking fluid everywhere. I don't have a brain. I don't even want to fuck. I just want to come.

"Meow for me," he says.

A kitten. What does a kitten sound like? A real mewl. No M sound, just a vowel. I make it. I mewl for him as he runs his fingertip over my hood, shifting it just enough. I mewl again. It's humiliating, to make animal sounds while tied and bent over, but it gives me something to concentrate on. This isn't the first time I've enjoyed being debased.

"Good girl. You're such a good girl. Do you want to come?"

"Yes."

"Yes, what?"

"Yes, please. Please. God, let me come for you."

With his free hand, he grabs the hair on the top of my head, yanking it against the ties to my ankles. "Don't move. Just meow."

He slides a finger in my asshole, and my mewl turns to a cry of pleasure. When he presses his thumb to my clit, hard, I lose my breath. He rotates the thumb, and I explode. My asshole pulses around him, my cunt tightens, and the rush of release comes out of my mouth in grunts that I can't concentrate on enough to make the kitten sounds he likes.

His thumb drifts off me halfway then presses again, and I explode all over, wiggling in the confines of the ropes. The orgasm is eternal, like an electrical pulse arching my back, my fingers gripping my forearms. He does it again, leaning forward and shoving two fingers in my ass. My back arches farther, and the ropes press into my ribs.

Time happens for someone else, but not me. The orgasm goes on and on under this madass bastard's hands.

I open my eyes, and I see him through my hair as he fucks me with his fingers again. His face is intense, as if he's reining in a hotblood, and I gear up for another explosion.

I need to breathe. I need to think. It's almost painful to come this much. But I can't move. I'm going to die, and live, and crack into a thousand fleshy pieces.

"Stop," I say. "Please stop."

"One more, kitten," he growls. And he gets it.

***

I rode the Westonwood sink on the tips of my right toes, sliding my wet pussy against it. I came in four pushes, legs tingling, back arching, mouth open. Knowing less than the sum of what I remembered and forgot, only blank, preciously empty but for pleasure.

CHAPTER 4

Margie, three years out of law school, was already boring. I couldn't stand her, but I loved her for sitting in the visitation room in a pale green suit, her red hair in a sensible bob.

Before I even had my butt in my chair, she said, "He's alive."

"How alive?"

"He's too weak to talk. You got the hoof knife between two ribs—"

"A hoof knife? My God—" Hoof knives didn't have a point, though mine was sharp on the tip. How hard had I been at him to get that to even puncture?

"You missed his heart by an eighth of an inch and just scraped a lung. There'll be a nice scar to show the grandkids."

"Was it me? I did it? Are you sure?"

"You called the cops and said you did, and you attacked them when they got there."

"I don't... There's no way I could have." I was utterly baffled. Why would I do that? I'd done crazy shit, but stab Deacon? That was the craziest of crazyfuckshit I'd ever heard. "Where? We weren't on Maundy Street. Couldn't have been."

"The stables. Then you tried to slit your own throat. You really don't remember?"

"You think I'm putting it on?"

"I wouldn't put anything past you." She held her face firm as if daring me to get offended.

"You don't have to represent me if you don't want to," I said. "I know you find me repulsive."

"I don't."

"You do. You've never understood me."

"That's not the same as finding you repulsive," Margie said. "Let's face it. *You* don't even understand you. The difference between us is that I happen to love you."

I had no answer. I just fixed my jaw and felt like more of a recalcitrant child than I ever did in front of Mom.

"Fiona, do you want to talk about this? Should I come back tomorrow? Or not at all? Daddy's trying to get me pulled off the case."

"Why?"

"He says I'm not experienced enough. I don't know the real reason." She shook her head. "Point is—"

I grabbed her hand over the table. "It has to be you. Don't leave me."

"Tell me what happened. I know you don't remember, but what was with you two? Did he cheat on you? Did he hit you? What would have made you snap?"

I rubbed my eyes with the heels of my hands. She didn't understand us. No one would.

"Drazen pledge," I said.

"I'm your lawyer. Anything you say is under attorney-client privilege."

I held up my hand. "Are you opening pledge or not?"

"Fine." She held up her hand. "Pledge open."

I relaxed. Between myself and my seven siblings, six sisters and one brother, opening a pledge meant nothing said could be repeated and only the truth could be spoken.

"This is so hard to explain," I said.

"It'll get easier after the first ten times."

"I don't know where to start."

She crossed her arms. "Start by not stalling. Assume I know you use drugs. Assume I know you've had more sex in the past three years than I've had in my life."

"We had an open-ish relationship."

"Okay."

"The ish part is that…" I swallowed. "Up until a few months ago, my other partners were limited to people we knew, at parties he threw." I didn't mention the knottings. I wasn't ready to tell her I had been a fuckable art object, because I'd have to explain that I'd never been in such control of my sexuality as I was in this open-ish relationship.

"And why did that change?"

There was a relief in her question, because it didn't judge the excesses, only the switch to normalcy.

"We fell in love." The blade of those words cut through the dullness of the meds, and snot and tears flooded my face.

"No," Margie said. "You stop right now."

I tried to tell her I couldn't, but I was beyond speaking, beyond using my mouth for anything but breathing thick cry gunk. I could barely breathe without croaking—how could I speak a whole sentence? "I couldn't have hurt him."

"Fuck." Margie had always been impatient with outbursts, yet she always knew what to do about them. She swung her chair to my side of the table as if she was flinging it in a bar fight and sat next to me, putting her arm over my shoulder. I fell into her. She said nothing and stroked my hair.

"He went away, and I couldn't keep it together," I croaked. "I have a hard time without sex. I need it. But he understands me. We worked on ways to make it work. Why would I stab him?"

"He's not saying. Is it possible he came after you, and you stabbed him in self-defense? Maybe he surprised you at the stables?"

"I don't remember. I swear I don't. What I was even doing there? I haven't been to Branwyn in forever."

"You have a chipped molar. Do you remember when that happened?" she asked.

"No."

"The exam showed nerve damage in your wrist. Did he ever grab you there?"

I shook my head as if I was emptying change out of the bottom of a piggy bank. Nerve damage to the wrist could be caused by an improper knotting, but Deacon would never, ever make that mistake, and I would have called it out if I'd felt a tingling.

"Margie, I'm so confused. It's like my brain isn't working right. I have to see him. I have to talk to him." I didn't know how I'd calmed enough to make sentences, but I had. I wiped my nose and smeared my tears over my eyelids with the backs of my hands.

"That's the least of your worries," she said. "You have to get released first. Your therapist has seventy-two hours to determine if you're a danger to yourself or others. So no more lunging over the desk to kill the good doctor. If you do get out, you'll get taken in for questioning or arrested, depending on what the DA feels he has and, to be honest, whatever Dad decides he wants to do. He's got every judge in L.A. in his pocket, but the media loves rich girls and violence. If you walk, it'll look like we've gotten away with attempted murder. And just so you know, we've got some problems at home."

"What?"

"Jonathan's girlfriend disappeared from a party at Sheila's last night. His car's gone."

"He had a girlfriend?" I tapped my fingers against my thumb, counting. When did my baby brother turn sixteen? How long had I been high on flake and fucking? Shit, he was old enough to *drive*?

"Theresa's friend Rachel."

Theresa was my sister, and Rachel was, indeed, her friend. She hung around a lot. I'd never given her a thought.

As if reading my mind, Margie continued. "I didn't know about her and Jon either. So that's why I'm here and not Quentin."

"I just want to talk to Deacon."

"I know. But maybe what you want isn't what you need." She took my hand. "When we're done here, you're having your orientation meeting with the hospital admin. Be nice. Be good. Okay?"

"Will being nice get me out?"

"It'll increase the odds."

"Then I'm all over it."

CHAPTER 5

The administrator smiled. She seemed genuine enough, but she was probably genuine with everyone, which made the whole act as fake as shit. Her brown hair was straight, but at the ends, I could see it was naturally curly. A little patch of eyebrow had begun to grow at the top of her nose. She wore a little wreath with a bell hanging from it on her lapel.

"I'm Doctor Frances Ramone, but you can just call me Frances."

Apparently, we were all on a first-name basis in Westonwood.

"You can call me Miss Drazen."

My joke had no effect on her that I could see. Being blind with a headache, who knew what was happening in my peripheral vision. On the other side of the glass walls, people played checkers and some asshole grumbled in a wheelchair. More windows decoratively barred against escape. Lightweight plastic chairs, great for throwing but not hurting. A television permanently set to beautiful scenes of nature, flowers, butterflies. And that was how rich kids disappeared into Westonwood. No TV. No internet. No phone.

"That's fine, Miss—"

"I was kidding. Fiona's fine."

"Are you okay, Fiona?"

Was I okay? What kind of question was that?

"I have a headache, and I'm a little grouchy, if you don't mind."

"Your medication's worn off."

Was her smile smug? Or just a smile?

"I need you to hear this and retain it, so I preferred you have all your faculties. Okay?" she said.

"Okay."

"You're here so we can determine if you're fit to be questioned for attempted murder, and if you had your faculties about you when you committed the act."

Though my crying was silent and controlled, Frances flipped me a tissue. I dabbed my eyes.

"Allegedly," I said.

"Allegedly. You have a lawyer you can discuss this with further."

"Yes."

She put a piece of paper in front of me. There was a list on it with little boxes to the left of each item, and she ticked them off as she spoke. "We don't allow you to use the phones or fax except to talk to lawyers. Even family calls come through us. We have some rules here, and the rules are tailored specifically for you. Everyone's comfort here is important. You will be provided everything you need from medicine to meals. You are not allowed any of your own. This is to prevent substance abuse. Do you understand?"

"Yes."

She ticked one of the boxes with her pen. I pressed my legs together and jammed my hands between my knees. I was so tense. I wanted to be in the common room having a goddamn conversation with the backgammon set.

"You will have two sessions per day with Doctor Chapman. He's agreed to keep seeing you, despite your attack this morning."

I nodded. I didn't like what I'd done. Not the attack on Deacon or Dr. Chapman. It wasn't *me.*

"Violence won't fly a second time. We don't like to use our solitary rooms, but we will if we think you're a danger to yourself or others. You're a compulsory patient, but we can send you to a state facility."

I looked her in the eye for the first time. Their color was indeterminate, somewhere between light brown and blue and green. She held my gaze.

"Is that what you told my father?" I considered telling her I'd go wherever my father wanted me, and if he wanted me in Westonwood, then that was where I'd stay. You didn't cross Daddy. Period.

She changed the subject. "There's a light switch in your room. It doesn't work after lights out at ten. Most residents go to bed earlier." Tick. "You will be given medication according to a schedule. You must take it as directed." Tick.

"I'd like an Advil or something." I needed a Vicodin, but I knew asking for it would get marked on my paper, and I wanted out, even if it meant getting questioned by the gestapo.

"After we're done here, I'll get you something for the headache." She tapped her pen, asking for attention to her list. "You will not touch any of the patients or staff." Tick. "Your bedroom door must remain open during the day unless your doctors or staff ask that it be closed." Tick. "You must get to your sessions on time. We consider punctuality a sign of your commitment to the process here. Two late appearances mean you are not fully committed." Tick. "And your performance in the bathroom this morning will not be repeated."

"What performance?"

"Specific to you, there will be no masturbation."

I laughed. "Are you *fucking* with me?"

"Next time we hear you through the door, we're coming in. We are a private institution. Accredited, yes, but we do get to custom-tailor the Westonwood experience to each patient. In your case, sex is a distraction that is strictly forbidden."

"Lady, I can make myself come by breathing a certain way, okay? And shame's not my thing. Privacy isn't a prerequisite; I'll come right in front of you. So that rule is a fucking joke."

"I assure you, it's not a joke." She slid back her chair. "Your meals are scheduled. Mark will take you to the dining hall."

***

Mark, the orderly, was one of those guys who was trouble outside his job. He had on the same pale blue uniform as the rest of the orderlies, but his goatee was fingered to a point and his hair was shaved over the ears. The top flopped down, but I knew he made it stick up on the weekends. I tried not to look too closely, but I couldn't help it. He had an empty piercing hole in his nostril. He glanced at me, and I turned away.

I held my tray in the center of the dining room, trying to decide between seats that all looked the same. The room was done up in modern grey and white, same as everything else. Even the Christmas decorations were simple brushed-chrome snowflakes hanging from the windows. The linoleum shined, the paint scuffs were removed nightly, and the chairs were Scandinavian, but it still looked and smelled like a mental ward.

A group of three ate on the patio. It rained on the other side of the overhang. They laughed and smoked cigarettes as if they were at the Wilshire Country Club, not Westonwood. They were my age, more or less, with smooth skin and trim bodies. One girl saw me and waved me over. I stood in the doorway.

"Fiona Drazen," she said. "Heard you were here."

They all looked at me. I waved. Their faces seemed familiar. The girl in question had her bare feet curled on the chair and a lit cigarette in the fingers that rested on her knee.

"Hey." One of the young men, with tight curly hair and a knowing slouch, raised his hand to me. "Good to see you again."

I didn't know him. Had I fucked him? Was I supposed to remember? I couldn't even remember the last two days.

"Hey." I nodded at him, then the rest.

The girl's shirt buckled under her crouch, and I saw the curve of her breast. I remembered her. It had been a weekend in her mother's time share—two days in an ocean of skin. I barely remembered their three faces from that party. Karen. Karen Hinnley. Her mother was a producer.

"Ojai," I said. "Fuck, man. What a weekend."

"It was…" She rolled her eyes as if at a loss for words.

"Beautiful," I finished for her.

"Damn," said the guy with the curly hair, "we should do it again."

"Yeah." Karen nodded to a boy with blond hair who couldn't have been a day over fifteen. "You gotta come this time."

Everyone concurred except me. I couldn't bear another minute. I didn't know why.

"Nice and quiet here," I said.

"Christmas," Karen said. "Everyone gets sprung for a couple of days. Except I don't want to go home to look at the buffet. Gross. After New Year's, there'll be a line for the tri-tip."

Too-Young shook his head. Curly Hair laughed. Warren. That was his name. Warren Chilton, son of the actor.

"I'm going inside," I said. "Call me when we're all out of here."

There was agreement, but no discussion about whether or not I would serve time, even though my situation must have been public knowledge. People like us didn't serve time. Even the suggestion meant that my lawyer wasn't connected well enough.

I wasn't hungry, so I drifted into the common room, where the TV screen showed nature in all its high-definition glory. It was compelling in its way. I sat on the grey leather couch and watched, staring at daisies fluttering in the breeze. I felt too weak for a walk. Frances had given me a cocktail of pills for the headache, some of which I recognized, and they dulled the pain and the brain.

I'd stabbed Deacon. What would make me do such a thing? What could he have done? Beat me? I laughed to myself, because beat me was what he did on any given day. I rubbed my eyes as if I wanted to erase the lids and see what I'd done.

My body tipped a quarter of a degree when someone sat next to me. I glanced toward my right. He had short-cropped hair and pink lips, and he smiled and blinked slowly. I could fuck him. No reason not to, besides the no touching rule and Deacon, who wasn't dead. I'd betrayed him enough already.

"*Bellis perennis*," he said, tilting his head toward the nature show. "Common daisy, often confused with their more tightly petaled family members, *Arctotis*. You're Fiona Drazen, aren't you?"

"Yeah."

"Jack Kent. Carlton Prep. I was a year below you. You were a celebrity even then. What are you in for?"

I didn't have a chance to answer before a nurse came close, and Jack pointed at the TV.

"*Arctotis stoechadifolia*, nearly extinct in its native South Africa, and now a weed pest in Southern California," he said.

"Attempted murder," I said when the nurse passed, "but I don't remember it."

"Car?"

"Knife."

"Wow. Trust you to do it big."

I wished I remembered this guy half as much as he remembered me.

"No, wait. I remember you," I said. "Nerd."

"Not totally unfuckable, I think. But yeah."

"What are you in for?"

"Being an embarrassment, unofficially. But officially, bipolar disorder."

"Picked up in a manic phase?" I asked.

"Totes manic. I came up with a new way to process *ricinus communis* in a hundred forty-seven steps. No one in their right mind could get past the seventy-fifth."

"Why did you?"

"Because I could. And the high? Woke out of it with my underwear full of jizz."

I nodded. I knew how he felt.

"You voluntary?" he asked.

I shook my head. The flowers changed from yellow to pink.

"Fifty-one-fiftied?"

"Yeah. I supposedly tried to stab a cop. Resisted arrest. Turned the knife on myself. Yada yada. I'm screwed."

"Who's your psych?" he asked.

"Chapman."

Jack puffed out his cheeks and released slowly, an expression of overwhelming sympathy.

"What?"

"Hardass."

"Really? Seems nice enough."

He shifted on the couch until he faced me, one leg bent on the cushions, the other with toes tensed against the floor. "It's his job to be nice. Listen. Do you want out or in?"

"Out, of course. What person in their right mind would want to stay here?"

"The question kind of answers itself. But if you want out, you have to do it in the seventy-two-hour window, six therapy sessions, or shit gets indefinite. Like, they keep you in thirty-day increments and revisit, and it gets less and less likely you'll get out unless your parents start making a stink. In my case, they won't, so I can stay as long as I want."

He didn't look at me for the last sentence, as if he couldn't bear the shame. I didn't blame him. I'd be ashamed too, if I had any.

"I'll convince him I'm sane."

Which meant I'd face charges. If I convinced him I was nuts, I'd be stuck in Westonwood with their no touching rule and scheduled meals. If I faced charges, would I get to see Deacon? Or would I just be out and arrested and as separate from him as I was in the hospital? Only he knew what happened. Only he could say what I'd done and hadn't done.

Staying in, staring at a flat screen of flowers with bars on the windows between Deacon and me, wasn't going to cut it. I had to take my chances with the real world, which meant no more tantrums. No more attacks on the doctor or anyone else. For the next two days, I would be a model citizen.

CHAPTER 6

"How was your morning?" Doctor Chapman—no, Elliot—asked. He had a tiny scratch on his left eyelid. Otherwise, he looked no worse for the wear.

"Fine," I said. "Sorry about attacking you. I'm not usually like that."

"You're repressing a slew of emotions and memories. Stuff can only stay in lockdown so long."

"Speaking of lockdown…" I curled my lip to the side. Elliot's hands were folded in front of him, and his attention was fully on me. I didn't know if anyone outside of Deacon had ever paid me such razor-sharp attention. "Is it even legal to have solitary confinement in a hospital?"

"I told Frances you needed an hour of restraints so you didn't hurt yourself. I didn't know how the tranq would affect you. Where did you get the idea of solitary?"

"She mentioned it. Like a threat. Not a fan of threats."

"What about the thought of it scares you?" he asked.

"I didn't say I was scared."

"Okay. Why bring it up? I'm sure she told you plenty of rules. Why does that stick out?"

"Because it's a legal issue."

"Is it?"

"According to Amnesty International and a whole bunch of entities who think it's wrong."

"We're a private institution serving a specific segment of society. We get some leeway," he said.

"Meaning there's enough money getting passed around that you can do what you want."

"Money flows both ways. But if you need reassurances, and you might, it's not something I'd sign off on for you." He watched me, reading me, observing me like a thing in a cage.

I wiggled in my seat, as if that would throw him off, but it didn't. The grip of his gaze only got tighter.

"You're making me uncomfortable," I said.

"You're not here to be comfortable."

How many times had Deacon said that when the backs of my knees bordered my face? Or when I didn't sit right at breakfast and he straightened me out?

"I hear you're a hardass," I said.

"As long as you contribute to your treatment, you'll have nothing negative to say about me. If you shut down or fail to participate fully, I will take note."

"That's hardassy."

He smiled, and his face curved from chin to forehead. Somehow, those two words had either delighted him or thwarted his expectations. I didn't know how to respond to his smile except to fidget and suppress my own grin.

"It's the world outside your bubble, Fiona. What you call hardass, other people call real."

"Where are you from, Doctor?"

"Elliot."

"Elliot. Tough Loveland? Toobad City? A mile outside Hardscrabble?"

"Menlo Park."

"Oh, sweet. Tech geek?" I asked.

"My dad actually knows how a microchip works. It's fascinating and utterly boring at the same time. I ran as fast as I could."

"To Los Angeles."

I could imagine him on the train in the middle of the night, running from a world where people found practical applications for calculus. He'd fail as a writer/actor/musician and put himself through school as a therapist, finding a hidden talent, yet always yearning to spend his nights with that one creative task that fulfilled him.

"Pasadena," he said.

"What's in Pasadena?"

"I went to school there. Let's get back to you."

He was evading. It had been all over his face since he mentioned the city where his school was. Would he lie? Were therapists allowed to do that? I didn't know if making our session about him would hurt my chances of release, but I wanted him to know if I could hold a conversation, act sane, function.

"Okay. Back to me," I said. "I've been to Pasadena. I was screwing a skate kid who ollied the six sets at Cal Arts. Did we meet then?"

"No."

"Pepperdine?"

"No."

"Four Twenty College?" I mentioned the name of the pot school, where one could learn how to deal marijuana legally, with a lilt in my voice.

He took a deep breath then, as if resigned, said, "Fuller."

"Fuller? That's a seminary."

"That a problem for you?"

"Did my father pick you personally?"

Elliot laughed again, rubbing the arm of his chair. "No. At least, I don't think so. But I'm aware that your family is, if not religious, Catholic in a way that's in the blood. I have no idea where you stand on it."

"I'm a C and E." I knew he'd know the term for Christmas and Easter Catholics.

"Why bother?"

"It's nice to touch base twice a year. Jump the hoops. You know, show face. So you're a priest? Or did you just say no to celibacy?"

"I'm Episcopalian, first off, so celibacy isn't on the table. And I just haven't been ordained."

"Why not?"

"This is really all going to be about me, isn't it?" he said.

"If you tell me why you're not ordained, I'll tell you something dirty I did."

I felt the weight of my mistake instantly.

He got dead serious. "I know that's how you're used to being valued, but that's not what you're here for."

"Sorry," I said. "It came out before I thought about it."

"That's allowed. There was some discussion with the board about whether or not you should have a male therapist, but from what we could understand, it wouldn't matter."

"So I got the hardass, unordained priest who knows I'm bisexual."

"You got the guy with the MDiv and PsyD who spent three years in a hospital chaplaincy in Compton. After that, I go where I'll do the most good, not where I get the most authority."

"Ah. Compton. You must have seen some bad shit."

"Very bad shit."

"Then why are you at the rich kids' retreat?"

"I can do good here as well as there." He wasn't thrown. Not an inch. I respected that.

"I need you to do some good for me," I said, feeling suddenly less vulnerable. "I want to go home."

"To Maundy Street?"

Trick question? Maybe. Deacon was on that private road. Second house to the right. First house on the right, his shibari students. Only house on the left was where the parties were. Where the art was made.

Where I surrendered to whomever my master allowed,
and my hunger was sated for days at a time.

"I figure I'll stay with my parents for a few weeks,
then decide. I mean, unless the prosecutor decides for
me."

"Will you try to see Deacon?"

"Why?"

"It could be dangerous."

"Dangerous?"

"I don't know if it's safe for you."

How much longer was this session? Because it
would take me that long to describe how fucking off
base he was. Despite needing to get the fuck out of
Westonwood, despite wanting to appear sane and
stable, I couldn't for the life of me let Elliot Chapman
misunderstand my lover.

"I'm more afraid of you than I am of Deacon," I
said. "I'm more afraid of this chair. The sky would fall
before he'd hurt me more than I could take. He is the
only man, the only person in the world who has made
me safe. And I mean, not safe from some boogeyman
or earthquakes or random shit happening. I mean I had
a place. I had things I had to do. I had rules. He was in
control, and the only time things got fucked up was
when I disobeyed him because I just had to fly off the
fucking handle. And before you ask, and you will, he
tied me up good. He gagged me and hit me. He made
me cry a hundred times, and he wiped my tears and I
thanked him for breaking me. I. Thanked. Him."

I expected my speech to disgust him, to give him cause to judge me, call me sick and out of control. Instead, he waited, expressionless.

"Do you want to remember what happened?" he finally asked.

"Yes."

"You might not be ready to remember."

"I don't feel right in my head. There are black spaces where feelings should be. Like someone came and erased stuff. I don't know if it was the drugs or the Librium you people put me on or what. I can't put stuff together. It's like I have the horse and I can see the track, but she's bucking, and the tack's in pieces all over the barn. Does that make sense?"

He sat back, putting an ankle on a knee, elbows on the arms of the chair. He rubbed his lip with his middle finger. "Have you ever been hypnotized?"

"You're joking."

"Best case scenario, you recall enough to release some of the pain you're in. Worst case scenario, you create a false memory that includes a unicorn and Jim Morrison in drag."

I laughed. I couldn't help it. That was the most ridiculous thing, and anything more ridiculous than what was actually happening deserved a laugh.

"Do I have to sit on the couch?" I indicated the long, uncomfortable divan behind me.

"Yes."

I didn't move.

"Come on," he said, standing. "It'll be fun."

"Are you going to make me cluck like a chicken?"

"It's just a relaxation technique. No more."

I took three steps to cross the room and sat on the couch.

He stood over me. "Lie back."

I looked up at him, a twisted smile on my face. I could fuck him. It should have occurred to me sooner. I was suddenly ready for sex, all tingling skin and hyper aware. I could sense his cock, its taste, its scent, its pink skin sliding against the silk of my thigh as it found its way home. It would feel so good, and if anyone needed to feel good, it was me.

"Lie back," he said again with a voice so devoid of desire, my own need collapsed.

I put my feet up and my head back. He sat next to me on the edge of the couch.

"I want you to recall the last time you were at the stables, okay?" He held up a pen, and I watched the angles of his fingers on the instrument. He didn't have a wedding ring. "Now focus on the tip of the pen." He moved the pen back and forth, and I fell into the rhythm of his breathing. His voice, a velvet mask of gentleness, said, "I'm going to count backward from five."

***

I feel a pressure on my hand. It's Deacon, slipping his hand into mine. The gesture, in its adolescent simplicity, creates a rush of emotions I can't hold back. I run out to the empty patio. There are candles everywhere from the cocktail hour, still flickering their last heated breaths. I've been without him for a week while he was on assignment, and now that he's back, he's a scary jar of emotion with a poorly threaded lid.

"Are you all right?" he asks, closing the glass door behind him.

"I'm fine, it's just…" I'm not good at expressing myself unless I'm angry, and I'm not angry. I'm just about everything else.

He takes me by the waist with his right arm. He's so tall, so handsome. His body moves like a leopard on the African plain. "Tell me."

"I don't think we should see each other anymore."

He smirks. He knows I'm not serious. He knows I'm broaching painful subjects by running away first.

"I'll be more than happy to blindfold you." He brushes his lips on my cheek. "But my eyes stay open. I want to see you beg for me later."

"I miss you when you're gone," I say. "I can't take it."

"Ten years ago, I'd have been gone for six months at a stretch."

When he says things like that, he reminds me of our age difference. Ten years ago, I was thirteen and he was almost thirty. I've never asked him what he sees in someone so young, because that would imply we have something more than a semi-casual open-hot-regular-fuck.

"Deacon, I'm sorry. I think now is a bad time, with everyone here." I push him off me and turn away from the strip of twinkling lights that disappears into the black of the sea. "We can talk later." I collect myself to pull him back to the glass doors.

I want to do a hundred crazy things. I want to grab a champagne bottle and down it. I want to stand on the railing and play at falling into the canyon. I want to get into my car and crash the gates. But he inspires me to be better than my impulses, and that's why I need him.

He yanks me back. "We talk now."

"You have guests."

"They don't need me. I can take you to the studio right now and knot you up and they'd be fine." His face gets hard. He becomes the man who spent years photographing the horror of central Africa, who took pictures and walked away. The man kept behind a rock for three months while he was negotiated out. That man, like a real face behind a mask, or a mask on real face, I can't disobey. "Talk,"

He doesn't have to threaten me. There's not a consequence in the world that would be stronger than his simple command. I don't fear him. He makes me strong. He makes me dare.

"I'm not one of those girls who's going to ask you where we are in a relationship," I say. "Because I'm not stupid. What we have is exactly what I want. I have you when you're here, which is most of the time. But if I want to fuck someone else, I just do it, no questions asked."

"As long as you stay fit and safe, kitten."

"My problem is, I'm starting to feel guilty about it."

He nods and looks down at our clasped hands. "I see."

"That's not the deal. We agreed. It's all clear, and it all works. But when you picked me up tonight…" I press my lips together and look out into the sparkling black skyline. "I wanted to run into your arms. I wanted to promise you my body and soul. Forsake all others. Beg you to make a commitment. And I wanted to run the other way and get high. Call Earl. Call Amanda. Fuck anything that walked. Fly to China to search for real opium."

"I can get you that."

"But you won't."

"Never."

"Why are we even this far?"

He laughs a little to himself then put his eyes back on my hand. "You…" He looks back up at me, eyes lit from one side by the light through the door and the other by the candles. "I'm not a jealous man. I've seen too much. And you, it was always a choice to share you or not have you."

"I know and—"

He cuts me off with a finger to my lips. "You did something to me. I was functioning, but I was in absolute despair. And you bang on my car window." He shakes his head. "You breathed life into me again. You gave me hope that everything on this waste of a planet isn't shit. You gave me permission to enjoy myself for the sake of it. I needed it. I needed you for that, and now, things have changed. We'd be crazy to pretend it's the same as it was two months ago even."

I know what he's asking. I want to sit, just to
relieve the ache in my heart that's traveled all over my
body, but I'm afraid to move.

"You want to do this?" I ask.

"Do you?"

Did I? What reason would I have to take him up on
a promise of fidelity? What was in it for me, except
him? "I've never been faithful to anyone in my life.
I'm not built for it."

He laughs. "You're built for a lot of things, kitten."

"I want you, Deacon. I want you so bad."

"I think we need this."

"I won't fail you," I say, believing it from
fingertips to core. I believe I can be exclusive to him.

"I know."

He leans in to kiss me, his breath a draft of mint
and the floral bloom of gin. I melt into his lips. My
face scrunches, and the ache in my body slams back
into my chest. I'm thrown by a bucking memory.

Fucking brain. Goddamn brain won't let me kiss
him. I'm on my bed in my stupid condo, weeping
uncontrollably, and my sheets stink to heaven of
fucking.

*Fiona. I'm not going to wake you. I'm going to
count to three. On three, think of your happiest
moment.*

I claw at the sheets until they rip.

One.

He is not the indestructible Dom. He's just a man. I
want to destroy the sheets, the bed, the room. In the
middle of my self-loathing, a weight between my legs

grows, a siren call to forgetfulness and obliteration. I throw a leg over the bed's footboard and ride it.

Two.

I cry out, and that cry is drowned out by the breaking dam of my orgasm.

Three.

I'm on a small plane, on my back. Charlie fucks me, and Amanda's face is right before me. Her tits brush my shoulder, her blond hair in my face. She smiles. She is beautiful. I open my mouth because I'm going to come. Charlie puts his lips on my cheek, grinding his sweet cock. Amanda's eyelids drop when I put my wet fingers on her clit. I'm high, on some delicious drug that lets me feel the connection between us three, our surrender, the tightening and expanding space between us, the puzzle pieces of cocks and cunts and asses, how we all fit together like one big universe forever and ever, amen.

***

I breathed as if my lungs had been vacuum-packed into my rib cage. Elliot moved to face me as I gulped air.

"I've never seen anyone have such an intense experience," he said.

"That's me. Intense experience girl." I grabbed his hand because I still felt as though I was falling.

He brought his other hand over mine. "You still don't remember."

"No. I'm tired."

His green-grey eyes looked at me as if they were peeling me open. "What are you feeling?"

"Tiredness."

"Don't shut down."

"I'm tired, and I want to…" I took a deep breath.

"You want to use."

"Yes. But I got it. It's not a problem."

"You're so sure? You haven't promised yourself this before? That you would stop using drugs or having sex to keep from feeling?"

"Don't push me. Please."

"It's my job to push you."

I leaned back and closed my eyes. I shut him out. He may have said something. I felt his presence in the room, his breath, his existence, his virility, and I closed myself to it completely.

CHAPTER 7

I didn't sleep in the dark.

I didn't really sleep, period.

I wasn't a *woe is me* kind of girl, because it wasn't as though I actually had problems. I didn't pretend I was ever going to live under a bridge. I didn't pretend bad shit didn't exist. I didn't pretend I didn't live in some wider world. I got it. I had a television. I had the internet. But what was I supposed to do? Devote my life to serving the poor? Take away all the suffering in the world?

But usually the minutes before sleep was when the woe-is-me cantered in, and if it was dark and I couldn't see something to focus on, they got bad. I hated them.

Your best friend died. You're in a mental ward. You nearly killed the only man who ever understood you. Half your life floated in a grey blur. Big fucking deal. Buck up. Fuck everyone. There was nothing they could do to me I wouldn't do to myself first.

Assholes.

Fucktards.

Animals feeding at a trough of fucking bile.

I didn't even know who I was cursing anymore, but fuck them.

I was fine. And when I got out, I was going to bathe in hundred-dollar bills and cocaine just to prove it.

I crossed my legs and blacked into an orgasm that was flat and rageful and over too soon. In the aftermath, I wept, because my best friend died, and I was in a mental ward, and I'd nearly killed the only man who cared for me.

Fuck me.

CHAPTER 8

"Your parents are in the waiting room," Elliot said when I entered.

"Should I go see them?"

"After the session."

"Making my dad wait?" I said, lying on the couch. "You're a brave man."

He seemed unimpressed with himself. "I want you to start with something pleasant," Elliot said, getting into the seat behind me.

I wanted to turn and look at him. Without seeing his face, the calm, dusty timbre of his voice was without flaw, and it soothed me, which made me anxious. I didn't trust my soothed, unregulated self. "I can just tell you about stuff. We don't have to do the hypnosis."

"Do you not want to?"

"Well, what do you want?"

"You have to make your own decision about how this goes."

I didn't trust my ability to make a decision. That had been my problem from the get-go. I could have just said that, but I was starting to think he didn't trust me any more than I trusted myself.

"Can you tell me why you like the hypnosis?" I asked.

"You have an anxiety disorder. We're medicating it, but the hypnosis backs up the relaxation without making you tired. And there's a time limit on how long you can be in here. I think we need to do whatever we can to move this along."

"I like all that."

"Okay, you can stop any time you want by saying a word."

"Like what? Like a safeword?" I wondered if he could see me smile.

"Sure. A safeword."

"Pinkerton."

"Pinkerton? The assassins of the old west?"

"The assassin of the 405." I didn't elaborate, because despite the slurry of medicine in my blood, I was going to cry.

"Okay," he said after I sniffled audibly. "I'm counting back from five, and start with something pleasant."

***

I'm horny.

The feeling hits like a freight train between my legs, before a scene or setting even comes into my mind. The swelling rush of blood to my clit begs for release. And then, the preoccupation. I have to get it. I don't care where it comes from. I need arms and legs all over me. I need to smell sweat, cunt, and sticky sperm.

This is the last thing you remember? Can you take me back a minute or two? What happened before?

Elliot's voice, in its pure perfection, doesn't break the reverie, but the realization that I was speaking aloud about the bite of my arousal certainly does. I tell him no. I'm not going backward, because the smell of wet cock and the subtle sting of cocaine fills my face. At this point, I have no idea what I'm narrating and what I'm keeping to myself, and I have no feelings about it either way.

I'm sitting on a toilet in a tiny club bathroom stall. Everything is marble and glass, but a bathroom stall is a bathroom stall. I hear the *thump thump* of music. The Pompeii Room. I look up. Earl. He's all right. Six-foot-four of pure stupid. Easy pickings. His dick is dusted with a fine powder.

"More," I say.

"Greedy bitch." He smiles and holds a baggie of coke over his erection. He taps a line onto it while I hold it level.

"I'm worth it," I say before I snort the line off his cock. Ah, that's just right, just that rush. The feeling of unmotivated pleasure exploding heart-to-brain-to-toes. I'm totally in control of everything in my line of sight, especially this fucker. "I'm going to suck your cock so hard your daddy's gonna come."

"Touch your pussy, baby," he growls.

But I don't. I won't ever touch myself, and this dumbass never remembers. I swallow his dick before he can ask again.

"Oh, fuck, baby—"

The music suddenly gets louder as the bathroom door opens, smacking Earl in the ass.

"Excuse me," the man in the dark suit says. He's halfway to closing the door.

"No problem," Earl says.

I look at the intruder in that fucking suit. He's really not a problem. He's more than good. More than tall. More than perfect. Dark hair and blue eyes. Rugged like a dock worker and refined like a prince. I have to stop him from leaving.

"Loosen that tie and get your cock out," I say. "I'm enough woman for two."

He smirks. "Sorry. I'm too much man for half a woman."

The door shuts, and the music goes back to a dulled *thump thump*.

"Snap," Earl says, aiming his dick at my lips again. "That was cold."

I have two choices: finish sucking off Earl and let him get me off, or not.

"Suck it yourself," I say, standing.

He grabs me by the neck. "Hey."

I look him in the eye. "Don't fuck with me, Earl. I say what goes and when. Jerk it off and make more." I leave before he can object, pulling my shirt together as I pass a short guy washing his hands.

The club is thick with humanity. The dance floor stinks. The voices are like a bag of broken glass. The music is a throbbing heartbeat. And the man is gone.

I put my hands on bare, sweaty skin, pushing through. Amanda finds me, blond hair stuck to her forehead, lipstick fading. Her bodyguard, Joel, is two steps behind her with his dark glasses and firearm. She kisses me on the lips. I push her away.

"You see a guy in a suit? Tall? Hair like this?" I make a motion with my fingers.

"Hot?"

"Hot."

She points at the exit with a wink. I smack a kiss on her lips and continue pushing through. She calls my name as I walk away, but I pretend I don't hear her. I have a man to find.

Nothing like coke to make the impossible seem within reach, or to make it within your rights to shove, growl, and curse through a crowd just to get a look at some hot stranger. Nothing like that expansion of the ego to make it okay to push some squealing teenybopper out of your way when she screams "Fiona Drazen! You're Fiona Drazen!" as if your name alone is front page fucking news.

Of course, they wait outside in a cluster, pressing against the red velvet ropes. Paparazzi don't care about the weather, which is rainy and cold for Los Angeles. Lights flash. They call my name as if I even answer to it anymore. Let them get their pictures. I have him in my sights.

He hands the valet a tip and takes the keys to a black Range Rover.

He is a thoroughbred, and twenty assholes with cameras are between him and me, which is too bad, because I have to have him.

I put my knuckles out to them, both middle fingers extended for all they're worth. I have rings on top of rings, and I know the lights will glint on them in the pictures. I'm going to look like a flashy rich bitch, and the coke tells me I don't give a fucking shit what Daddy thinks.

I turn to the doorman, a skinny ex-cop with a pencil moustache. He looks at my chest then at my face. I know Irv. He's a hustler. He keeps these assholes off us, but he takes their cash to let them know when Amanda and I show up.

"Irv! What the fuck?"

"I got it," he says.

"Outta my way, cocksuckers!" I plow through them with Irv's help.

They back off for him in a way they'd never do for me. I know they'd chew me up, spit me out, and photograph me crawling to the hospital. I get to the Range Rover and pound on the passenger-side window. It's tinted. The car doesn't move, and the window stays up. Do I have the right one?

"Fiona Drazen!"

They're behind me, and I'm on the curb, out of Irv's field of influence. If he comes to get me, he's leaving the door, and that's not cool. I pound on the window again. Bursts of light flash on it.

I'm about to get mobbed.

"Hey, asshole," I shout.

The window rolls down so slowly, I feel as if I'm in a movie about falling.

And there he is. My heart jumps out of my chest.

"Hi," I say, sticking my head in. I feel them behind me. I hear them calling my name, over and over. "You took something of mine outta the bathroom."

"Really?" He's older than I thought, and that makes him more attractive then humanly possible. "What?"

Fiona.

"My heart." It's a stupid come on, but I'm a girl. I can get away with it.

I'm going to count backward from three. At one, you'll open your eyes feeling rested and relaxed.

"Ah. I thought maybe your shirt buttons."

For the first time, he glances at my chest, and I feel that my breasts are chilled. My shirt is wide open, diamond-studded nipple rings glistening. Fucking Earl with his octopus hands.

Three.

"Don't make me turn around," I say. "They already got enough pictures."

Two.

He takes a second to think about it, looking me straight in the face. A little smirk plays on the perfect line of his lips, and I think I just might die.

One.

cd reiss

CHAPTER 9

I was barely in the Westonwood waiting room before Mom hugged me fiercely, all defiance and no affection. It was amazing how much strength was in that tiny little bag of bones.

"It's fine, Ma." I looked over her shoulder at Dad, his Drazen-trademark red hair just beginning to turn grey.

His hands were in his pockets and his shoulder was against the wall. I rolled my eyes at him, but he just turned to look out the window. He always tried so hard, and I always failed him.

Everything in the room was designed to avoid upsetting the patients and their families. Round table in pale blue Formica with matching water pitcher and three plastic glasses. White molded plastic chairs with chrome legs. The windows were barred in the same decorative pattern overlooking the expanse of the Topanga Canyon, which was covered in grey, misty rain. The seasonal decorations were non-denominational. The best seat in the house, for the benefit of the people writing the checks.

Mom squeezed me, and I felt something hard and breakable between us. She pulled back and handed me a wrapped gift. Dancing snowmen. Gold ribbon.

"I had it in case you came to the house."

I popped the tape and unfolded the paper, revealing a framed photo. "Snowcone." I pulled it from the wrapping completely. I stood in my riding gear, all of fifteen, next to my beautiful grey stallion. "Thanks, Mom."

"Lindy says you haven't been to the stables in a long time, at least not before the other day."

I hadn't ridden Snowcone in how long? Was it measured in years already? The last time I'd gone to the stables, I'd gone with two guys I'd promised to fuck on a hay bale. I was so high, Lindy kicked me out. Told me I wasn't worthy of the labor animals. I cursed her, knowing she was right.

"We're going to get you cleared of all this," Mom whispered. She looked me in the eye, squeezing my shoulders. "Ten years ago, we could have made it go away. But the internet—" She shook her head. "You're a good girl. Your father and I know you didn't do this."

Daddy didn't look so sure.

"Thanks, Mom. I'm fine."

"We're going to get everyone on this. This man? This Deacon Bruce? We'll get so much dirt on him, pressing charges would ruin him."

"Eileen," Dad said, "it's not like pushing a button."

She turned to Dad, giving him the fire-eye. The power struggle between my parents had always been epic. One day, one of them would die in a pile of crushed bone shards and twisted skin.

"What's it like then?" snarled Mom.

"Quentin's dealing with the other matter right now—"

"He can do both."

"No."

A staring contest ensued. I didn't know if they were going to kiss or scratch each other's eyes out.

"Guys?" I said, but I had no effect on their stare. "I'm going to get out in a few days. Can we—"

Without breaking their staring contest, Dad said, "Don't bet on getting out."

"But—"

"She's getting out, Declan," Mom said. "I'm calling Franco. If you want to handle it that way, I'll handle it that way."

"You won't. She doesn't need the kind of help you're offering."

I didn't know what they were talking about, but I knew that if Mom wanted to call Franco, whoever that was, she was calling Franco. My part in the conversation was pretty much over. "Thanks, guys. Nice visit. Merry fucking Christmas."

I turned on my soft, suede heel and strode out. Halfway down the hall, Dad caught up to me.

"Thanks for defending me," I said. "I think."

"Hold up." He stepped in front of me, blocking my path.

The security guard stood from his station. My father looked at the two-hundred-pound refrigerator of a man, who carried a gun, and with just a look, made him sit the fuck back down.

Dad turned his blue eyes to me. "This pleases you? What you're doing?"

"I'm not here to shame you."

"The effect is the same, but I know that was never much of a concern for you."

"Just tell me what you want."

He held his hand up before I could finish. "Your life is out of control. You've wrecked more cars than I've bought. You've used your body shamelessly. I can only imagine what your blood is actually made of. And you've never faced a single consequence. You have a classic case of affluenza."

I crossed my arms. I didn't know if he was making a joke or not. "You're saying I'm a bad person."

"You're dissolute, and you don't care."

"And you do?" I stiffened, and my extremities tingled. You didn't challenge Daddy. You just didn't. If I never faced any consequences in the outside world, inside his fiefdom, I certainly did. Yet there I was, feeling safe enough to do just that.

"I do. This family, Fiona, this ten-person unit, is all that matters. How we're perceived is important. How we act is important. And if you don't get control of yourself, I'm taking control."

That was close, too close. I heard his words in Deacon's voice, and I squirmed.

He continued, poking at my core insecurity. "Whether or not you ever leave here can very easily be up to me."

"I'm of age," I whispered, but I knew I had no way of enforcing my emancipation.

"Indeed you are. Something to think about. The dew is off the petal, and you've gone from wild child to aged curiosity. There are younger and wilder taking your place as we speak."

Maybe my medication was wearing off or maybe I was raw from recalling my first meeting with Deacon, but something about him calling me old and washed up frightened me. Something about the look on his face, as if he'd stepped in a hot mess on the sidewalk. I respected my father, respected his opinions and beliefs even if I didn't follow them. I had consistently thwarted his will, and he'd consistently bailed me out because I had such respect for him. What would happen if that respect went away? Would he stop protecting me?

"What about you?" I shouted, though he never flinched. "What about what *you did*? You shamed this family with Mom."

"I married her. No one's marrying you." He didn't bat a fucking eyelash.

The only reason I didn't lunge for him was he was telling me the truth.

Instead, I walked toward the hall. Like a cat, he moved so quickly and silently, I was surprised when I felt a yank at the back of my collar. The security guard did exactly nothing when Daddy took my jaw in his hands.

He whispered in my ear, "When are we going to stop playing at this same drama, Fiona? It's tiresome. And I don't like disruption."

There was only one answer.

"Yes, Daddy."

"We understand each other then?"

"Yes."

"You will get control of your life?"

"Yes."

"Good, because if you don't, I will. And you will not like it."

***

I couldn't bear the common room, the patio, the garden. Couldn't stand a conversation. My parents confused me. I always left their company wondering what the fuck had just happened. So I took my meds as prescribed and went to lie down.

You're controlled by your cunt. Who controls your cunt, controls you.

The ceiling of my grey and white little room was a dull shade of neutral. The shade was drawn over the open window, and when the breeze came, it slapped against the sill as if angry.

I control my cunt.

Deacon in his suit, smiling that godawful devil of a smile, looked at my face even though I was naked and tied to hooks in the wall. He didn't believe me. He was right. In the battle for control of my life, my cunt won every time.

I'll control it, kitten. And you're welcome. He put the riding crop to my lips, and I kissed it. *It's three days. You'll be good, or this is what you're getting.*

I put my eyes all over his handsome face, which I wasn't supposed to do. I was supposed to look at the floor as a symbol of my submission. He drew the crop back and whacked the side of my face with it. The sting felt wet and deep.

That's to keep you in the house. He said it without cruelty or emotion, then backhanded the crop over my breasts. *That's for looking me in the eye.*

The next ten came down in a rain of blows over my belly, my hips, the tops of my thighs. Then, with an underhanded swat, he slapped my clit with the leather. I ground my teeth. I wasn't supposed to scream.

That's three days of control I expect.

I remembered the welts when he touched them, the way they burned as he unhooked me and threw me on the bed, lashing me face down to the bedposts so that the mattress rubbed them when he fucked me. I remembered the orgasm spilling out of me, and the welts bleeding over the next three days, reminding me of how hard I'd come that day. And how without him, I had no control over my cunt.

You can touch yourself if you want, but that's it.

He smirked like Satan. I didn't even address the joke of it, I was so aroused. I didn't touch myself for pleasure, even when he tormented me by giving me that as my only option.

Thinking of him in my Westonwood bed, my clit felt like a hot, throbbing marble. I crossed my legs under the covers, listening to the rain in the palm trees outside. I played the memory over again and again. The pain all over my body, the sweat in the wounds as I danced at Dabney's with who-even-knows. Earl's fingers digging in them as he fucked me from behind. I took his friend Tammy's pussy in my mouth, the sting of flake hot on my tongue. I knew he'd punish me when he got back.

When Master Deacon came home three days later, the beating had been relentless, and joyful in its way. He'd tugged and twisted on my nipple rings until I came, then made me come again and again. It was the beginning, and a game. Our hearts hadn't dropped out of us yet.

Yet.

I pressed my thighs together, rotating my hips slightly. It would take forever to come, but I wasn't going anywhere. My lips parted, and heat washed over my hips, my heart beat between my legs, and I felt that relief, that joy, that release.

CHAPTER 10

Lunch.

I felt as though I was being fattened for the Easter feast. It was Asian today. Dumpling soup, fried rice, Korean beef, some lightly sautéed green leafy vegetable with a name I couldn't recall.

"It's low-sodium soy sauce," said Karen from the seat across from me. She'd had her face buried in her journal while her soup got cold. "I guess they figure you're on so many meds the sodium might spike your pressure?" She dumped a stream of soy sauce on her fried rice. Her hair was twisted up in a quick knot, and her swan-length neck had a fresh hickey blossoming on its base.

"You wanna cover up the suck stain?" I touched my neck.

She looked shocked then tried to look at her own neck, as if that was possible.

"There's a mirror right over there," I suggested.

"No, I got it." She took her hair down.

Seeing her hair against her face and her forearms up, I realized how thin she was. Jesus, I must have been stoned on scrips yesterday. She fiddled with her fork and glanced at Mark, the orderly who moonlit as a nose-ring-wearing punk. I noticed from that he had a tattoo creeping onto his neck from under his collar. He looked at her and spun his finger as if telling her to get to it. She picked up her fork. I knew from the way she handled it that no food was landing in her mouth. I'd seen that particular twirl before.

"I'm sorry I didn't make Amanda's funeral," she said. "There was so much going on. My sister was there. Tanya. She went. Said it rained. Like a movie." She rolled her eyes.

"It's all right. Nothing really happened. You know. Closed casket from the accident. She didn't zombie." I raised my arm and curled it at the wrist, making an ugly zombie face, because what better way to pretend I didn't give a shit?

"I heard about the party after," Karen said.

"Yeah." I cleared my throat. "Wow. Days. It was the best sendoff I could have given her." I felt bad scooping food into my face in front of someone who was obviously anorexic, but I was hungry. "We had a line of limos up the hill. Man, there was so much flake."

I stopped chewing and pushed my tray away. The flake had been the problem. At that point, Deacon didn't care that I'd had multiple partners. He cared that he didn't know them. He cared that there had been drugs on Maundy Street, where he wanted things quiet and unimpeachable, and he cared that I'd taken them. He wouldn't knot me until it was out of my system and then some. That week had been torture. Amanda's death had weighed on me fully, and Deacon withheld every coping mechanism I had.

"I spent a week in the corner drooling after that," I said as if it was a joke.

But it hadn't been. I'd felt like the bottom was going to fall out of me until Deacon picked me up and knotted me from the ceiling. Things had changed after Amanda died. It was as if we needed each other, he and I. As if it pained him to see me take such poor care of myself. It wasn't too long after that we decided to own each other.

"Hey," Warren said, sitting across from me. "Rain just stopped. Creek's flooding up to the bench."

"There's a creek?"

Warren and Karen glanced at each other.

She pushed her tray forward and shot a look at Mark before standing. "Let's give Fiona a tour. Our tour."

Warren looked me up and down, as if seeing my body through the light blue cotton uniform. "Can I trust you?"

"You can take your tour and stick it."

"You want this tour," Karen said. "It's worth it. Almost as good as freedom."

"I don't need to prove I'm trustworthy. I ate you out in Ojai, and you"—I turned to Warren—"licked flake off my tits. That was my coke, and you never gave me shit in return but numb nipples."

"Point taken," Warren said as he guided me out the door.

The outside had been designed, manicured, and planted to the teeth. The verdant garden was dotted with wood benches—places to reflect on your mental sickness, eat yourself with regret, and chew on your shortcomings. Jack crouched over a bed of wildflowers, rubbing the yellow petals.

"Hey, Jack," Warren said as he slapped the not totally unfuckable nerd so hard on the ass he nearly fell over.

"Ow!"

"Not cool, Warren," I said, helping Jack up. "You all right?"

"I'm fine." He glared at Warren.

I brushed Jack's shoulders even though there was nothing there.

"Sorry, man." Warren made a fist as if to punch Jack in the arm.

Jack flinched. I liked Warren less and less with each passing second.

"We're checking out the holes. You coming?" Warren asked.

"Nah. I'm good."

"Can we go?" Karen asked, walking backward toward the gardens. "I have a session in fifteen minutes." She indicated the clock on the highest part of the common building.

Our personal effects had been taken, including watches. The clocks dotting the facility were the only way we had to keep time.

"Me too," I said.

Warren jogged ahead of us and spread his arms. He looked handsome in the deep foliage, like a Greek god of abundance. "There are cameras everywhere." He pointed upward.

I didn't look directly, but with a sidelong glance, I saw the shiny glass at the crook of a tree branch.

"But there are some corners they don't get to. Holes in their vision matrix." Even in his silly mental ward uniform, Warren carried himself as if he was entitled to the known universe. He stood with his back to an old oak. "Like here. Hole. Right here. They might find you if they're walking around, but the cameras can't see shit until they prune this shit back. Follow me." Like the docent of sneaky spaces, he pointed out three more places where a patient couldn't be seen by the cameras.

"But they know where the holes are, too," Karen interjected. "If they see you go out of range, and don't see you come out, they come and check."

"If they're paying attention," Warren said. "Which is a crap shoot. Let's go to the creek."

We walked down a winding path. I heard cars speeding somewhere past a hedge, but it didn't sound like a major road. The sound of moving water added to the white noise, and past a line of trees, we came to a swelling creek. A chain-link fence separated us from it.

"Is that PCH?" I asked, referring to the water. I followed them along the fence to a hole cut into it.

"Not even close." Warren pulled the cut fence open. "We're in the middle of nowhere."

We crept through. Karen put her journal on a fallen tree trunk and kicked off her shoes. She rolled up her pants.

"Go on, sweetheart," Warren said as Karen stepped into the water. "I'm sitting this out."

"Why?" I followed Karen's lead, rolling up my pants.

"The thing with my kid brother."

"What thing?" I put my toe in. The water was ice cold, even in the sun, and the bed was made up of small, rounded rocks.

"I waterboarded him." He said it as if he'd helped the kid color or taught him how to play a video game. "They catch me in water, and my dad's gonna kill me."

"If it's morning, they can't see much once you're in the water. The lenses get condensation on them, and the cameras get wet. If it's just rained, the leaves are heavy and block the cameras." Karen held her hands out and put her face to the sky. "I love the holes."

"If you're ever looking for Karen," Warren called from the edge, "check the holes."

There was something freeing about not being seen by the hospital staff, but with Warren's eyes on me, I didn't feel safe.

"What are you looking at?" I said.

"You got Chapman?"

"Yeah."

Warren craned his neck to see the clock at the top of the common building. "Next set of sessions starts in five."

Fuck. I hopped out of the water and got my cold feet back into my shoes.

"You know how to get back?" Karen shouted, but I was already past the chain link.

CHAPTER 11

Doctor Chapman looked tired as he closed the blinds against the sun.

"Why did you stop me last time?" My feet ached from the cold water, and I was trying to hide that I was winded from the run over. "There was a good part coming up."

"The session was over." He glanced out the window and back at me so quickly, I might have missed it if the Adderall hadn't made me hyper vigilant.

"Really?"

"Why do you ask?"

"Because we had five minutes of small talk after that. So, you know, I kind of left thinking about what happened after. In Deacon's car."

"You can tell me." He rubbed his upper lip again.

I saw his watch peek past his cuff, hanging on his wrist. He had nice wrists, angled and wide. Masculine.

I narrowed my eyes, willing his cuff back so I could see more.

"I don't want to tell you now. Your loss," I said.

"Your parents came to visit last night. How did that go?"

I shrugged.

"Your father's an interesting guy."

"How so?"

"He married your mother quite young."

I sat ramrod straight, and I felt my hand want to go up, as if fending him off. That was sacred territory. He could psychoanalyze me all he wanted, but my family was off limits. "They're still married eight children later. I don't see the problem."

He said nothing. As much as I wanted to scrape his pretty little face off for it, I wanted to prove myself even more.

"You going to hypnotize me again?" I asked.

"If you found it helpful last time."

"You ever going to take a stand on something you want, Doctor?"

He stood. "Not in this room, no. In this room, you're the boss."

Well, if that was how it was going to be, I would take it. I could be the boss of this tiny, half-lit room. I threw myself on the couch. Elliot followed and sat behind me. I heard the rustle of him crossing his legs.

"Counting backward from five," he said.

"Okay."

"Five."

***

His car is huge, and he smells like peppermint. He doesn't say anything, and my chest winds up with tension. Is this a mistake? He doesn't look like a serial killer, but maybe he's not interested in me. Earl is a good enough fuck in a pinch; that would be better than nothing.

"Got a name?" I ask, trying to get my shirt buttoned.

"Yes."

"My name's Fiona."

"I figured that out." He turns his head a little. "I'm Deacon." His eyes drift down to my exposed tits then back to the road.

"Should I bother buttoning up?"

"Yes."

I shake as I finger the buttons. That wasn't the answer I expected, and I'm suddenly ashamed. But when he flattens his hand on the wheel and turns it with pressure on the heel, my nipples harden through the white shirt, and the rings piercing them stretch the fabric.

"So," I say, "where we going?"

"Away from a crowd of paparazzi." He stops at a light and turns toward me. "How do you live like that? All these people around all the time?"

I shrug. "At first, I got upset when they misunderstood something or printed me kissing a Brent Ogilve when I was dating Gerald. That sucked. But then, Gerald was kind of a dick, so they did me a favor."

I don't want to talk about paparazzi. I want this guy. I put my hand on his thigh and slide it between his legs. He's all muscle. He puts his hand on mine and moves it back to my lap.

"Are you gay?" I ask.

"No."

"Look, if you don't want to do it, that's fine. Just drop me off."

"Take it easy," he says, squeezing my hand before he lets it go.

But I'm uncomfortable, unhappy. The car feels too small, and this man expands like a balloon, as if his psychic space crowds me. Suddenly, I don't want to have sex at all. Not with him, not with anyone. I just want to feel like I have everything under control again.

I open the door enough for the hood light to go on. We're not going fast, and I know he'll slow down. But he doesn't. He stretches over me and pulls the seat belt across my body. His peppermint smell is layered with sandalwood, and I want to fall inside it at the same time as I want out of this fucking car.

Snap. He clicks the belt. "You're in the arts district. It's late, and everyone's drunk. There's no need to take unnecessary risks."

I'm pissed. Really pissed. Because he's right.

I look at him as he drives a few blocks. I hate him, and I'm attracted to him, and in my rage, I want to fuck again. I feel the swell between my legs as I remember shit I'm trying to forget—that windshield kiss, and me in the passenger seat inches from a dead girl's pussy, and it smells like sex.

I'm not thinking about that.

I am *not* thinking about that.

Fiona, do you want to stop? You're crying.

I say something. Something about Pinkerton never failing when Amanda drove. And no, I don't want to fucking stop. I want to remember Deacon with this level of clarity and beauty. Something about the way he smells and the texture of his jacket in the lamplight. Something about his hands. The way they're completely still when he isn't using them. I'd forgotten that.

I feel Elliot's fingers on my wrist and hear the soft curtain of his voice.

All right. You're mixing things up. Amanda Westin died after you met Deacon. You don't have to think about the accident if you don't want to. You're in control.

Deacon turns right then right again onto a cobblestone loading dock. We're in an unlit alley downtown. He turns on the dome light.

"So," I say, "what do you want? You going to tie me up and kill me?"

He laughs, and my anger melts off me.

"I'm assuming that wasn't your boyfriend."

I shrug. "Just a Thursday night."

I undo the seatbelt to see if he'll let me. He makes no move to restrain me again. I turn around and kneel on the warm leather, the small of my back to the dashboard, to get a good look at this guy. Older. Late thirties, early forties maybe. Little beard happening. Strong chin. Dark hair. Eyes blue and lit from within.

I know he can see my tits through my shirt. I go braless pretty often because I'm small, somewhere between an A and a B. I call it A plus. My light pink nipples are standing on end from him looking at me.

"You like what you see?" I ask.

"Yes, quite a bit. Do you always walk around half naked?"

"Only when I chase gorgeous men out of bathrooms."

"And why did you do that?"

"Impulse and instinct. It's how I do everything."

"You're very beautiful," he says.

"Thanks, hon. You don't need to flatter me to get under my skirt."

"I'm still trying to decide if it would be worthwhile."

"Oh, I promise…" I reach out to touch him, but he grabs my wrist.

"Put them behind you, on the dash."

Oh. A bossy one.

"You came into the bathroom," I say. "Do you still have to pee?"

"I'm good."

"Uh, huh. I don't know what you're into, but I've done that."

"You let someone piss on you?"

"It was a give and take."

"And how was it?"

I shrug without moving my hands off the leather dash. "Scratched it off my bucket list."

He takes half a pause before he laughs so hard and deep I can see his chest moving. I can't help but smile. Pleasing him does something for me.

"How old are you?" he asks.

"Old enough."

He's perturbed by that answer, and he snaps up my bag.

"Hey!"

"Hands on the dash," he says while looking in my bag.

He flips past my packet of birth control pills and extracts my wallet. I'm nervous, like Sister Elizabeth is standing over me with a napkin and I have a wad of gum in my mouth.

"This your kink?" I say. "Looking in a girl's bag?"

He flips my wallet open. "You seem quite willing to let me use your body, but you don't want me to look in your bag. I don't know if the boundary differences are cultural or generational, but the fact is, I want to keep myself out of jail if you don't mind." He rifles through the wad of hundreds to the stack of cards. The Amex Black has a quarter inch of white dust on the edge. He presses his thumb to my driver's license and pushes it out. "Twenty-two."

"My birthday's Groundhog Day."

He tucks my license back and puts the wallet back in my bag. "What else is on that bucket list of yours?" He tosses the bag aside.

I bite my bottom lip. "Getting nailed in an alley downtown."

"A real one."

I would have gotten bored with this shit already, but I want to impress him. I want him to *like* me. "Ride dressage in the Olympics."

"Dressage? I would have taken you for a dancer."

"What's that supposed to mean?"

"It wasn't meant as an insult. You have a gymnast's body, but the discipline that takes would keep you out of club bathrooms. So I went to dancer. Dressage wouldn't have occurred to me, even if I knew you rode."

"I was the only rider at Stanford with an Arabian. And I ride him Prix St. George." My answer is defensive, not sexy. He's implied that I'm an out-of-control little girl with a flat chest and muscular legs. Normally a man's little insults are met with backhanded returns ending in ammunition for dirty hatefuck talk. But I want this man to respect me.

"Calm, forward, straight," he says, putting his thumb to my cheek. "And submission to the bit."

"You've ridden?"

"I spent a few years overseas with a certain crowd."

I turn my head and take his thumb between my lips, letting it slip past my teeth and over my tongue. He smiles when I suck it on the way out.

"I'm going to be honest," he says.

"Uh-huh." I take his thumb again.

"I'm not looking for a sex partner."

"Then what were you doing at Pompeii?" I take his middle and ring finger down my throat, all the way, and watch his face change. He may have just wanted to help a celebutante in distress, but his ideas of what to do with her are expanding by the second. I see it in his willing, wet fingers and the dilation of his pupils.

"Meeting the owner. We're scheduling an event," he says.

"What kind of event?"

"Something you might enjoy."

And my brain, in its super-relaxed state, fell into his smiling blue eyes. At that event in the house on Maundy Street, I would be on my knees with an expert tongue in my asshole, a vibrating object in my cunt, and my mouth on a cock. So happy, content, satisfied, that when the orgasms came, I felt as if I'd transcended my own skin.

***

I woke with my back arched, out of breath, with Elliot pressed two fingers to the inside of my wrist.

"I'm sorry," I said, panting.

"Don't be." He stared at his watch another second then put my hand down. "You're taching at one-fourteen."

"I wasn't trying to make you uncomfortable."

"You're going to have to work harder than that to make me uncomfortable." His smile was so relaxed, I believed him.

I wanted to work hard enough to make him uncomfortable, just to see what he looked like. "I'll remember that."

"Just lie back and relax."

We didn't say anything for a few minutes. I breathed slowly, trying to slow my racing heart.

"Was that your first encounter with Deacon?"

"Yes."

"When did you see him again?"

"He invited me to that party through Paolo, the owner of the club. I wasn't going to go, but Charlie heard it was at Maundy Street and went nuts. I figured I'd see Deacon again. Which I didn't."

"No?"

"He's known for not showing to his own parties. But he found me, like, a week later at Lucien's. Bought the whole table dinner from across the room then tried to slip out."

"What did you do?"

I huffed a sarcastic little laugh. "Chased his ass. He was waiting for me in the parking lot, like he knew I'd come after him. And he wouldn't let me touch him. Even back at his place. He said touching him was a privilege that was earned. I didn't understand. I thought he was just being a dick."

"Many dominants don't like to be touched. At least not before there's trust."

"Yeah, well, I didn't know that. How do *you* know?"

"I'm treating you. I've stayed up late doing a lot of research."

"'Research,' huh? With a box of tissues by the computer, I bet."

He didn't answer.

"Sorry," I said.

"When did he let you touch him?"

"I don't know. I keep thinking, if I stabbed him, he must have been tied down or something. But how? He'd been tied down in Congo, so he's not turned on getting tied up. He's anti-aroused. So maybe I ran up and jabbed him?" I shook my head slowly. "The last thing I remember is a jumble of shit."

"What kind of shit?"

"Pills and sex. And some rope work. I think I was suspended for part of whatever it was. Which means Deacon was there, and I was the one tied up."

"No one else ever tied you?" Elliot asked.

"I got tied up plenty, before we were exclusive, but the real rope work, the art, the shibari? That was all Deacon. He wouldn't let anyone else do it. And that was from the beginning."

"So in a way, you were exclusive from day one."

"In a way." I hadn't thought of it that way, and I swelled with a childish pride. "Even Martin and Debbie weren't allowed."

"Who are they?"

"They live in number two. They're his top trainees. Debbie's great. She only ties men. She does beautiful things, and she's really methodical, even for how young she is. Martin's talented, but Deacon says he'll never really get it." I shrugged. "Even if I was so stoned I'd let them knot me, well, Debbie wouldn't have disobeyed, and Martin was in New York. So I don't know."

Elliot shifted a pen on his desk as if it was a lever he needed to flip, then he shifted in his seat. Why was his every movement so interesting to me? Why did I watch him? It could have been because he had so much power over me, or it could have been because he expressed himself with his motions, as if a shade of what he was about to say existed in his body before it came alive verbally.

"I think we're going to find out soon," he said. "Mister Bruce has been found well enough to be interviewed. So if you have anything to tell me, the police, or your lawyer, you should do so."

He was well enough to be interviewed. He was getting better. I swallowed hard and took a deep breath. "Thank God."

"You're not afraid of what he's going to say?"

"No."

"He may implicate you."

"I'm not worried about it."

"What are you worried about?" he asked.

"How long have you been working here?"

"That's not relevant right now. Not as relevant as you changing the subject."

"My point is, no matter what he says, we have lawyers. Our lawyers have lawyers. If Hitler needed to walk, Hitler would walk. What I'm worried about isn't the law. Deacon is my law. He's the only one I have to obey. I'm worried about what I *did*. How it affected *him.* Us."

kick.

"You have a very strange sense of entitlement."

"I'm told it's affluenza."

He smiled ruefully. "Session over. See you tomorrow."

CHAPTER 12

I could have eaten in my room, but I wasn't good at alone time, and I'd already had a bit too much of it. So when Jack sat next to me, I was relieved by the human contact. At the same time, I didn't know what to do with it.

"Last day is tomorrow," he said, breaking his artisanal bread and dunking it in his sweet whipped butter. "What's your guess?"

"I think they're going to let me out."

"You'll get picked up before you're out the door."

I shrugged. "They'll set bail. I'll go home, and then we'll see."

Split pea soup with hand-cut bits of ham. Grilled vegetables. Marinated tri-tip. All the meals had been like that, and by "like that," I meant the very worst of what I'd ever had in my life, unless I was deliberately slumming or in a neighborhood south of the 10.

I pushed my tray away. "This food sucks."

I wanted something, but it wasn't on my tray. The roil of anxiety built in my chest. I had no relief for it, at least not in the pills they were feeding me. Not in the therapy or hypnosis. I had ways to manage myself, and they had all been taken away.

"They're going to expect me to be sober when I get out, aren't they?" I asked.

"Probably. But whatever. Just get someone else to drive, and they'll never know the difference. No one gives a shit what you do as long as you're not hurting some middle-class honor student. Then you're up shit creek."

The way he rubbed his bread around his bowl, as if he was just flipping off some commentary, should have told me he didn't mean it personally. He wasn't trying to jab at me. He wasn't trying to twist my sore places. But he did, and I decided it was careless and cruel.

"What's that supposed to mean?" I said.

He barely stopped eating. "Means we can get away with self-destruction until we hurt someone who doesn't have anything. Then it's off with our heads." He drew his finger across his throat. "Seriously, I'm in here because I sold an ounce of sky gum to a teacher. The news was all about how much my dad made versus how much she made. And I'm like, seriously? I sold four grams to Rolf Wente, and I got crickets." He stopped chewing. "Why are you looking at me like that?"

"People cared about Amanda."

"No. You cared. The rest of them were slowing down to see the blood on the road."

kick.

There had been plenty of it. Rich blood. Blue blood if you counted Charlie's cut head. Amanda's flowed with the webbed lines of windshield cracks as I sat in the passenger seat in a half daze. I thought she looked like a cartoon character sticking her head through a wall, and she'd just pull it out and make a goofy face. I put my hand on her ass and patted it, whispering, "Tight and sweet, baby. Tight and sweet. You're going to be okay."

"You're not going to cry," Jack said, incredulous. "You're not allowed to have problems, sweet tits. Sorry."

I didn't know what was going on with Jack. Something must have been happening in his world, because he was ornery and defensive, but I didn't care. The thought that no one had cared about Amanda dying, even though it had been in all the papers and her parents turned people away from the funeral, pulled at my heart. He was right. No one cared about her.

And how did you make people care? Amanda Westin died in a drunk-driving accident, and the driver walked away because his dad was a duke in some tiny European backwater, and the news vans came, and the flowers were imported from India, but how could I make them care? Tell them who she was? That she made me laugh when I was sad? That she loved her dogs? That she gave me the last of her flake when I needed it? Or that she stood by me the million times I bailed on her to get laid?

"She was a good person," I said. "One of the best."

"Sure." He shrugged.

That little knot of anxiety grew into something bigger, something without boundaries. It was larger than me. Wider than the expanse of my chest, with an energy all its own.

It was that force inside me, but not *me*, that flung my tray. Flinging it felt good, because it made a little room inside me, a tiny corner without anxiety. I flung Jack's tray. I swept my hand over the table and knocked over the condiments, and then I got up on the table. When I flung myself off it, the motherfuckers were already there to catch me. Bernie, good old Bernie, looked intent on not letting me fall, and Frances already had a needle.

CHAPTER 13

I woke up strapped to the bed. Elliot sat by me, marking something on a chart.

"Oh, God," I said, trying to put my hand over my eyes and failing.

Elliot got up and turned off the overhead, flicking on the soft table lamp over my photo of Snowcone. "Do you have any muscle pain or weakness?"

"What drugs did you give me? I can't feel anything."

"Do you promise not to get violent?"

"Fuck. You're never going to let me out now. I'm stuck here. Why did I do that?" My face crunched up. I was going to cry right there in front of Elliot, every tear another nail in the coffin of my sanity. When he freed my right hand, I put it over my face.

"I'm not an MD, so I don't dispense your meds, I only suggest. But it looks like you got a little too much slap and not enough tickle," he said.

"What?"

He laughed. "I'm sorry. It's late. My sense of humor shorts out when I'm tired." He freed my left arm and went to the foot of the bed.

"Nice you have one that's wired at all."

He smiled as he unstrapped my feet. "I'll contraindicate the Paxil."

He got my ankles free, and I sat up. The world swam a little, and I gripped the edge of the bed. The room righted itself.

"Are you going to let me go?" I asked.

"I have another day of observation. You want to go?"

"Please."

He sat next to me. "Deacon Bruce, by his own admission, fell on the hoof knife."

"He what?"

"Fell on the thing twice, apparently."

Any relaxation I'd gotten from the meds molted off me like a skin I'd never owned. "He's protecting me."

"The district attorney doesn't believe him either. But in the end, it'll be hard to make a case. You're a lucky girl." His green-grey eyes looked at me as if they were peeling me open. "You don't look relieved."

"I'm relieved."

"Don't start packing yet. Okay?"

"I don't have much to pack. A picture, and I guess there were clothes? I mean, who knows with me, right?" I held my hand out for the picture, and like a father intuiting what his toddler wanted, Elliot gave it to me.

"You're going to have to continue some sort of program once you're out," he said. "I know you guys have ways of getting around it, but for your own good, I hope this is the bottom for you."

I barely heard him. I was looking at myself with my new horse. I'd gotten Snowcone as a surprise from Daddy, and my delight in my new black-and-white dressage gear was all over my face. Snowcone was pulling away from the odd, smiling creature at his feet.

"How old are you in that picture?" Elliot asked, sitting in the chair by the bed.

"I'd just turned fifteen. Mom didn't want me to have him. She thought I was too irresponsible. I swore I was going to prove her wrong."

"Did you?"

"I did, until recently. When Amanda died, I kind of left him to the stable. Fuck. He was mine; I trained him. He was so good. Perfect temperament, moving off my legs easily, finding the bit like a champ. And I just abandoned him as if he didn't even matter. And I want people to care about me? Fuck, I am worthless."

Elliot handed me a box of tissues, and I had to laugh through my tears.

"Fucking therapists," I said.

"What?"

"Like the most important thing in the world is giving me a place to put my snot."

He leaned forward, elbows on his knees. "The most important thing is that, by doing that, I show you you're not worthless."

I blew my nose. I felt so bad, as if a rotting, twisting ball of blackness curled inside me was getting bigger by the minute. I knew how to push it back. I knew how to manage it, and watching Elliot's fingers woven together between his knees, I started wondering how to get him into bed. When his hand touched my forearm, a blazing heat fell between us.

"You were out for the morning session. So our last one's in an hour."

He needed to stop touching me. He needed to back the fuck off. I had to swallow my reaction to him like a horse pill.

"Okay," I said, not looking at him.

I knew his eyes would be warm and inviting, and his lips curved like a promise. He smelled of musk and desire. His fingers slid a quarter inch over my skin when he removed his hand. When he walked out, he took the air with him.

Oh God.

I was swelled.

I needed it.

If I went into Elliot's office like this, I would do something stupid. I would lose control. Touch him. Get close to him. Show him my body. And that would be it. I'd be stuck in Westonwood, because despite the heat I felt in his touch, he was a professional. A therapeutic fuck wasn't on the table. My brain might have been high on fuckjuice, but that didn't make me stupid.

An hour. I had an hour to get unswelled. I was in a mixed-gender ward with sixty minutes to find willing, slightly sane cock. How hard could it be?

In two days, I'd gotten the hang of the schedule, more or less. I went into the rec room. It was off hours, meaning most of the residents had therapy or visits. Jack wasn't in front of the TV cataloging flowers. Karen was outside, scribbling in her journal as if homework was due.

"Looking for something?"

I spun around. Frances stood behind me with her hands behind her.

"I was. Uh, Jack's usually hanging around here?"

"You might check his room."

"Yeah, thanks." I stepped back.

"Miss Drazen," Frances said.

"Yeah?"

"The doors stay open."

"Yes, ma'am."

I scuttled off toward the hall that led to the rooms. After I made the first turn, I doubled back to the garden. The rain had disappeared for a full day, and rainy-ass Los Angeles was sunny-ass Los Angeles again. I looked for someone, anyone. I drifted over to the creek, thinking maybe Jack was picking up nettles or something. He wasn't, but Warren Chilton was. His eyes cut through me from the other side of the fence.

"Hi," I said. "Whatcha doing?"

"What's it look like?"

"Jerking around." I poked my head through the hole in the gate. "Want help?"

I came out on the other side just as Warren tossed a rock into the creek. It got lost in the rushing swells without even a splash.

"They kill you with boredom in this shithole," he said.

"Got a cure for that," I said, taking his hand.

I put it on my breast, which was usually a non-event, considering their size. But Warren, without missing a beat, grabbed the nipple and pinched.

"These were pierced," he said.

"They took everything. You know that."

He twisted. God, it felt good. I didn't like the guy, but I liked how he was making me feel.

"I'm going to fuck you so hard you're going to have to stay here another ten years."

"Get to it, preppy."

He searched my face for a second, as if discerning whether or not I was looking to trap or double-cross him. I moved my hand to his cock, which was at least half hard. God, I hoped his meds didn't make him unable to do it, because I had no time to work him. He grabbed me by the neck and pushed me against the fence.

"Wa..." I couldn't finish the word, such was the pressure on my throat.

I didn't like it, and I wanted to tell him to stop. When I tried to push his arm away, he ignored it and yanked at my pants.

"Keep still," he said, fingering my cleft under the standard-issue panties. "Oh, you're ready."

His grip on my neck moved to my upper chest when he got his dick out. I breathed.

"No choking, Warren." I pulled one pant leg down. "I'm warning you."

"Sure."

"Hey." The voice wasn't loud, just firm.

Fuck. A guard stood behind us. Warren jumped back as if his hand had been in the cookie jar, but I could have told him he hadn't even gotten the lid off yet.

"What are you doing on that side of the fence?"

"It was her." Warren pointed at me, the fleshy rod swinging from above his waistband making a lie of his participation.

"Chilton, get the fuck out of here," the guard said. "Don't make me write your ass up again." He got out his walkie-talkie, observing the hole in the fence. "Hey, Ned," he said into the radio. "There's a breach at four-seven-two."

Warren ran through the hole and past the grove of trees. The guard glanced at me after I'd gotten my pants up.

"Go on inside," he said. "You get a pass this time. Go on."

He indicated the building, and I hustled. I had forty-five minutes left. My clit rubbed on my inner thighs when I hustled back inside, swelled to pain and wanting release so bad it swallowed my brain. All I could think about was fucking. Fucking swell. I hated my needs. For the first time, they seemed more of a burden than an indelible character trait.

Warren was a dead issue. That asshole was going to mark me and get me in trouble. He must have been the source of Karen's mark.

When I got back to the residents' hall, I realized I had no idea where Jack's room was. Fuck. Fuck fuck fuckity fuck. Was he even in his room? And what if I couldn't find him? I was starting to think about Elliot in ways I shouldn't. Ways that would come out in hypnosis. He'd touch me again, and I'd say something like, "Hey...let's—"

I ran down the halls, looking in each room. All the doors were open. Most of the rooms were empty, or being cleaned, or occupied by strangers. In forty minutes, I'd be in front of a man, and he had a dick, and I could maybe convince him to fuck me.

But I kept thinking about being tied to the ceiling, the knots in the rope rubbing my skin, and Deacon's cock sliding against the back of my thigh.

Tell me how badly you want it, beautiful kitten.
Bad bad bad bad....

My ass. My poor ass as he'd paddled it, holding back the avalanche of need. I lost days to his ministrations. I needed him. I had no control without him.

And I'd stabbed him.

I didn't believe his denials for a minute. His refusal to implicate me only meant one thing: I'd done it. I'd stabbed him.

What the fuck?

What the actual *fuck?*

"Hi, Fiona."

I spun. Jack was standing in the hall with a paper towel of yellow petals.

"Jack, I was looking for you."

"Job well done, then. You found me."

I stepped close to him so I could say something without being overheard. "You said you weren't completely unfuckable."

"I'd like to think so. Why?"

It was as if the cues and clues I'd given men my entire sexual life were a foreign code to this guy. Normally I'd reveal some part of my body, but we were on camera.

So I tilted my head and pressed my lips together before whispering, "I want to show you how fuckable you are."

His bottom jaw went slack, and his eyes widened. He made a little tick in the back of his throat as if an attempt to swallow had failed. I took that as a good sign.

"Do you want to touch my tits? The nipples are hard already. I know places we can go to do it, where they can't see. I can put your cock down my throat so deep I can lick your balls. And I'll swallow your load, every drop."

He didn't say anything, and when I went to touch his arm, he dropped his paper towel, sending yellow petals adrift.

"Jack?"

He ran down the hall as if his ass was on fire.

I guessed I had that coming. It was a mental ward, after all. But talking dirty had made the swell worse. I had thirty minutes to release it, and I didn't even have a damn vibrator. I was going to just going to have to take care of myself and hope for the best.

My room was a few doors down. I ran in and closed the door. The window was still open, and the shade blew in, slapping back against the window when the breeze went out. I went into the bathroom. Frances didn't want to hear me, I got that. I knew I could be quiet. I'd done it for Deacon a hundred times.

Slipping out of my crazy-proof cotton pants and shoes, I eyed the sink again, its smooth texture and cold surface. It was good in a pinch, but this wasn't a pinch. This was something else entirely. I wanted warm skin and a fullness, a filled feeling.

There were reasons I didn't touch myself. Good reasons.

That pleases you, Fiona? What you're doing?

That was old stuff. Dad catching me in the chair by the window.

Because it's disgusting.

He'd been behind me, arms crossed, having watched the whole thing in the reflection of the window. I was spread-eagled on the chair, seeing how long I could make myself go. I was fifteen, and so unsure about the power of my feelings and my bursts of uninitiated arousal.

I knew one of you would be like this. Out of seven, the odds...

I hadn't reached orgasm yet when he let himself be seen, and when I jumped up in the chair at the sound of his voice, I was still aroused.

Outside the bathroom, the shade slapped against that open widow.

A hundred years ago, you'd have been married off before you shamed this whole family. But now? Now I can't do a damned thing. I'd like to sew it shut.

I didn't think about the other thing.

The thing where he was erect.

I couldn't forget it, but I didn't think about it. I kept it in some nether-place where it existed without me actually seeing it or letting it come to me in words.

I sat on the toilet and opened my legs, angling my body so the pressure of the lid rubbed on me. That wasn't going to work. Fuck. I wanted my fingers, their warmth, their shape, their knowing touch.

I could put a tampon in without trouble, and I could groom and wash myself. But I hadn't touched myself to orgasm since Daddy had walked out of the room, shaking his head. He'd never lectured me afterward, and I never found out if he mentioned it to Mom. Mom, as if sensing something was amiss, stayed close, and defended me from any and all consequences. But he could pit us against each other. I became the one my sisters should avoid emulating. The bad example. The dissolute one. I lived it joyfully, believing they all envied me.

But God, straddling that stupid toilet, I just wanted to fuck. So bad. And there was no one in this shithole. Elliot would know; he'd see the swell on me. I'd do something impulsive, and I'd have to stay.

But I needed it, and I wasn't using the word "need" loosely.

I was about to get up and just go figure it out when I decided to give in to impulse. I slid my middle finger over my clit.

I gasped. The shade slapped against the window again, and something fell. I'd forgotten how good that was, how electric. My finger and my clit reacted at the same time, and I was blindsided by it.

The bathroom door opened. I jerked my hand up and opened my eyes.

Mark, the orderly with the tattoo, said, "Whatcha doing?"

"I'm in the bathroom, asshole."

He stood there, taking up the doorframe. He had Jack's paper towel in his hand, a few yellow petals poking out. "Bedroom door was closed."

"Maybe you know why now?"

"Sure do." He still didn't move

My eyes drifted where they always did when I felt that constant throb between my legs. He had a cock, and if it wasn't hard, I'd be a monkey's uncle. I could take that thing. It would have to be a secret for all of how many hours? I'd go to my session, clear shit up, get rubberstamped, and get the fuck over to Deacon, aye-sap.

"There aren't cameras in the bathrooms, are there?"

He looked me up and down, eyes lingering on my bare legs and the triangle where they met. "On the doorway. Everything up to the toilet."

"Too bad. I was feeling like a fuckdoll." Newly emboldened, I stroked my belly with an extended finger.

"Five minutes, pretty thing."

"Three's all I got."

He winked at me. "Stay right where you are." He clicked the door shut behind him.

I had twenty minutes. Maybe I could be two minutes late to the session. I had no idea who reported lateness or at what point they'd come looking for me. I wasn't interested in getting found with Mark.

I sat back and let my fingers rediscover pleasure. I didn't think about anything, just focused on what I was feeling. I teased the swell out so that when a real living, breathing cock entered the room, I could get the job done. I needed it, and with every pulse of need, I shifted my finger over my clit. Sweet, overwhelming delight. Thoughtless anticipation, the tremble of life, a precipice into the chasm of forgetting.

And he was back.

"What did you do?"

"My buddy's at the monitors." He closed the door. "Get down, psycho."

He took me by the back of the head and pulled me to my knees. I yanked his waistband down and pulled out his cock. It smelled antiseptic and stung my tongue when I licked it.

"Oh God, yes, you little fucking whore. Take it all."

I looked up at him, making my eyes big and wide. I let him slide his dick over my tongue and down my open throat. He held me there a second longer than I thought I could stand it.

I stood up. "Just fuck me. Use me. I'll be your horny slut. Your fuckdoll whore."

He turned me and pushed me against the toilet. I braced myself on the tank. He got a condom on while I stared at the tiles. I hoped he didn't try anal. That was always nice, but I wouldn't come without help, and I suspected he wasn't a big helper. He jammed it in my pussy and held onto my hips, pumping in and out. I angled my body so his shaft rubbed my clit, and I felt the orgasm coming.

"Oh, fuck you, you little rich slut. You like it like this, don't you? You like it when I fuck you like this."

"I'm a whore. Fuck me like a whore. Yes, fuck me like a rich little whore." I knew I was saying the right things. They turned me on, and they made him slam me harder. I felt the swirl of my climax.

Everything was there. Skin on skin. Tick. Prone, exposed to a stranger. Tick. No commitments, no intimacy. Tick. A little risk thrown in for good measure. Tick, tick, tick.

There was the thing I'd forgotten.

The boredom. The space between the hunt for sex and the orgasm, and even the orgasm, half the time. Tedious.

I wanted to come and get it the fuck over with. The seconds in between were not savored but reviled. They were an unworthy means to a worthy end. His grunts were annoying. His dirty talk held no meaning. I didn't want to look at him, so I bent over. He thought I was a slut, so he called me a slut. Boring.

I pushed against him. "Harder, fucker. Bury it. Break it off."

He slapped my ass and pounded me. "Shut up, bitch."

His balls slapped my clit, and his dick plowed against it. I was going to come. I felt it in my muscles, and when they tensed and clenched, it was a release, not a joy. Just a job well done.

He came with an *oof*, and I rolled my eyes.

He stroked my back from neck to ass. "Baby—"

"Get out. I have shit to do."

"Why's it gotta be like that?" He got the condom off and rolled it up in toilet paper.

I stood up. "How else should it be?"

"You don't want me to be nice?"

"You thought you were the one using me? Funny."

"You some kinda weirdo?"

"You're in a mental ward, dude. Come on. Get the fuck out of my bathroom."

Condom stowed in his pocket, pants zipped, girl disinterested, he got the hint and opened the door. He was almost out, but being a man, he needed the last word.

"Slut."

CHAPTER 14

"Last session," Elliot said. "How do you feel?"

He looked relaxed, clean-shaven, happy. I hadn't realized how troubled he'd looked during our last session.

"I'm okay. Are you going to let me go?"

"I can only make a recommendation. After this session, I'll type it up, and we'll meet with Frances and your lawyer. Give me an hour after we're done. Your mother and lawyer are already here."

I sit on the couch. "Are we doing hypnosis again today?"

He shrugged. "Sure, if you're up for it. I'd like to try to find more recent memories. Track back to the last thing you remember."

I laid back. "We tried this before."

"Maybe things have changed." He sat next to me and got out his pen.

I wished I could have met him under different circumstances. When he was a seminarian, before I was a happy little fuckdoll, when things could have been kind of normal. That absurd sense of humor would drive me insane while my affluenza frustrated him.

"Things have changed," I said, though I couldn't define them.

"Keep your eyes on the tip of the pen."

***

Are you relaxed?

I am. I feel a freedom I hadn't felt before. I feel hopeful and generous, sweet and melancholy. Emboldened and encouraged, ready to start a new journey, a life after this incident.

I want you to think about the ride here, to Westonwood. Can you remember that?

I don't. It's not even a blur; it's blank.

Go back a little further. To the stables. You were given a shot. Do you remember the pain in your arm?

The black goes grey, and I feel something in my arm, as if I'm being poked with a rigid finger. I feel something else, a pounding in my chest, a confusion that I'm separate from. I can't tell what's happening, besides the feeling of being restrained.

Go back further. Before the shot.

I don't want to. I feel the resistance binding me to my forgetfulness, the comfort of not knowing. If I lean into it, just a little, maybe I can see what happened without feeling it. Maybe I can observe coldly, like a reporter noting facts for relevance, not profundity. If I let myself accept that fear, I'll know. So I relax into where the rope of my fear pulls and binds me, dropping into some unknown graphite-colored place in my head. I expect to go back in my memory a minute, two minutes, half an hour, but intuitively, though I can't tell the whens and wheres, I know I've gone back further.

His breath falls on my cheek, and a pain in my arm runs from my wrist to the sensitive side of my bicep.

"You did not," he says from deep in his throat. He's naked, stunning, the stink of sex and blood on him. He pins me to the wall, the friction screaming against the open skin on my ass.

Regret. Pounds of it. Miles wide. Regret to the depth of my broken spirit.

"I'm sorry." Am I? Or am I just saying it?

"Why?"

My wrist hurts. He's pressing it so hard against the wall, as if I'd leave, as if I'd ever turn my back on him. Yet I want to get away, to run, to show him that I can abandon him the way he abandons me.

I wiggle, but he only presses harder and demands, "Why?"

"Get off me!"

"Tell me why!" His eyes are wider, his teeth flashing as if he wants to rip out my throat. "Why?"

"I need it!"

The words come out before I think, and they're poison to him. Before I expect it, he slaps me in the mouth. He lets me go, and I fall to the floor. When I look at him, he's cradling the lower half of his face as if he can't believe what he's done. He's slapped me plenty, but not in anger. Not without me halfway in subspace and high on dopamine. Never outside a scene.

But that's nothing compared to what he does next. The ropes of my fear try to pull me away, back to safety, and I let them.

What is it? What does he do?

I must have been silent too long. I must have watched Deacon's face, frozen in my memory, for a second too many. The sense that he is going to do something terrible is all I have, but I don't remember what it is. When Elliot asks from the present what Deacon does, I stay to see it.

"I'm sorry," Deacon says.

I don't say anything. My face hurts, and I taste liquid copper. We stay like that forever, or time is stretched in my memory. This is the moment I can tell him it's okay, or the moment I can be angry, or I can have a reaction that will make him not do what he's going to do.

But I don't do anything. Not a word or gesture.

He walks out.

I don't know why there's a finality to it that I haven't ever felt before, but there is. When the bedroom door clicks behind him, that's it.

I want to wake up. I don't want to observe my emotions, even as a time-traveling bystander.

You're fidgeting.

Pinkerton Pinkerton Pinkerton

Okay, on three, you'll wake rested and happy.

Amanda's next to her hot pink Bugattti. Pinkerton, before it became the assassin of the 405. She tips, holds herself straight, smiles at me. Oh, no. I don't think so.

One.

I snap the keys from her and give them to Charlie. I open the passenger door in the front, even though it's her car. Let her sit in the back. I don't want her puking on Charlie when he's driving.

Two.

I'm not in the mood to die.

Three.

***

"You associate those two things," Elliot said. "Amanda dying, and Deacon hitting you."

"He hit me all the time. It was a turn-on."

"Hard enough to break a molar?"

I heard him shift in his chair. I wanted to sit upright, but my body felt like the inside of a broken egg.

"Did you usually sit in the back of Pinkerton?"

"If Charlie was driving and it's Amanda's car, I should be in the back. That's just social mores. But Amanda got aggressive when she drank too much, and she was doing God knows what else. I just didn't feel like worrying about her having a psychotic break while

Charlie was driving, because it wasn't like he was in much better shape."

"And Deacon hitting you?"

"He left. That was the painful part."

"Why did he leave?"

I sighed. It had been the sore point between us. Our thing. "He went away for a few days to hang a show in San Diego. And I swelled, so I needed to fuck, and I got it where I could. I tried not to. I tried to be good, but I failed, okay? And he found out, which was lying on top of cheating. I packed my shit and left. That was the last time I saw him. Until the stables, which I still don't remember."

"So you feel responsible for him leaving?"

"I was. We stopped sharing and fucking around. We agreed."

"I think you need some therapy after you leave here. I don't think you've worked through your feelings. We haven't had time to touch on anything in your past."

"Sure, Elliot. Sure."

"And I know you don't have access to the outside world in here, but the press is being unkind is probably the nicest way to put it. You're going to need somewhere to go to talk about it."

"I'm sure I can find someone."

"It's been nice talking to you, Fiona. I'm pretty sure I know what you think of yourself, but I want you to know that you don't have to believe it."

I twisted around until I could see him. He looked the same as always, relaxed and confident, middle finger on his upper lip as if he couldn't think without it.

"Believe what?" I asked.

"That you're useless."

"You don't know what you're talking about."

"You're sensitive. You're bright. You're brave. Can you believe that?"

He pissed me off. He had no right to tell me about me, not after three days. But if I argued with him, if I put him in his place, it would be another reason to let me rot in that grey room.

"Thanks, Doc."

He stood and opened the door. "I want you to remember that when you see your mother. She's in visiting."

CHAPTER 15

Margie caught me in the foyer, on the way to the visiting room.

"Have you seen Mom?" I asked.

"I have no idea what she's doing here. I told her to stay home. Jonathan's a wreck over his girlfriend, and Theresa's no better. They're mad at Dad, but won't say why, which is fucking typical Drazen bullshit. You sure you don't want to stay in here?"

"I'm sure."

"Between you and Jonathan, the press is going apeshit."

"Fuck them."

"I wish I could get myself committed. " Her phone dinged, and she tapped it. "Hang on, this came from the prosecutor." She scanned the email. "Provided you're cleared to leave here, you agree not to contest the charge and waive the preliminary hearing. We accept aggravated assault. Community service. I'm inclined to tell him to fuck off. Deacon's denying it all, so bail and a grand jury appearance is my guess."

"What does the press want?"

"They want you turning on a spit."

"Take the plea."

"As your attorney, I wouldn't advise it."

I shrugged. "I'd rather not have this over my head. Or have Deacon change his mind after I see him and beg forgiveness. Just take it and be done. A little community service won't kill me."

"As your sister, I approve."

I sneered at her playfully, and she hid her smile.

***

The garland and lights were gone from the visiting room, as if Christmas had been mentioned once and wiped away. Mom paced in front of the window, a wisp of a thing with a bent neck, tapping her finger on her chin.

"Hi, Mom."

When she faced me, I knew she wasn't there to join me for the therapist's recommendation. Her eyes were on fire, her jaw set. She sat down like it was her job.

"What's happening?" I asked.

"How are you?"

"I'm f—"

"Did your father ever touch you?"

"Mom!"

"Answer me!" She slammed her palm on the table.

I held my hands up and sat back. It was too much. I needed time to think, to talk to people. To breathe, for Chrissakes.

"Fiona, tell me. I'll protect you. I'll put myself between you and anything. But just tell me. Did he ever touch you in a way that made you uncomfortable?"

"No, Mom. He never touched me inappropriately."

"Your sisters?"

"Why now? I'm twenty-three years old. What happened?"

She sighed then pursed her lips, a series of facial tics that meant she was holding in an emotion, any emotion. I said nothing. My heart was pounding too fast.

"There's talk that he'd had a relationship with the girl who just died."

"Jonathan's girlfriend?"

"Previous to that, when she was a bit younger, but yes. Your brother didn't know until recently, and he's not happy with it. So." She sat up straighter. "Did he ever touch one of your sisters?"

I wished for time, and my wish was not granted. The clock still moved. Things had been said in pledge. We'd held our hands up and made promises, and though I'd broken plenty of promises in life, I'd never broken pledge. None of us had. We had a code of silence, and inside of it sat our denials, our shame, our bonds.

"I can't say," I said. "Not directly."

Mom's face melted, constricting, as if her tears shrunk and crinkled it. I snapped up the ubiquitous box of tissues and put it in front of her.

"So it's true," she spit out before the sob choked her.

"It's complicated, Mom. It's not what you think, but I can't say. It's not my place."

"You think you're protecting someone, but have you thought that the way you all are… that you hurt each other with this wall you put up?"

"Yeah, I've thought about it."

"What are you all afraid of?"

Afraid? I wasn't afraid of being cut off from their money. I had more than I needed, and it couldn't be touched. I wasn't afraid of being cut off from my siblings, because we were strung together with strong twine.

I was afraid of Dad.

Dad had a way of making things happen. He had a way of using his relationships and his money to create chaos or order, as he saw fit.

But Mom was in distress, and how much worse could it all get? I was already up a creek; what would be the difference if I threw my paddle in the rushing billows of shit?

"You should talk to Carrie," I said, instantly regretting it, yet feeling the release of something I hadn't realized I was holding so close.

"It was Carrie?" she squeaked.

"Talk to her."

She wiped her eyes, but her tears barely abated. "God damn that big house." She folded and refolded the tissue. "God damn the corners. You can't see what's happening. You can't hear. We avoid each other. Did you see how that happened? How we went to the far corners?"

"There were eight kids, Mom. You needed a big house. What were you supposed to do?"

"Pay attention. I was supposed to pay attention!"

Mom looked up and behind me. I followed her gaze.

Margie stood in the doorway. "What's going on?"

"Nothing," I said. "Mom thinks I'm a disappointment and a failure." I may have been ready to break pledge, but I wasn't ready to get busted for it. "Let's get this done. You're buying me dinner at Roberto's. I'm hungry, and I need a drink."

"You're too young to need a drink," Margie said, getting out of the way of the exit.

"Well, I need something."

"How about a job?" she replied, putting her arm around Mom.

I stuck my tongue out at her.

CHAPTER 16

We waited.

On the hard, squared-off modern couch in the common room, we waited. I imagined Elliot typing, his middle finger rubbing his upper lip. I waited for Mom to come back from the parking lot and throttle me into saying what I knew, which was nothing. I swear, I knew nothing except that Carrie had talked to Deirdre and Sheila about something in pledge. That was it. Nothing I could build a case on.

I shook a little. I was getting out. The press was out to skewer me and possibly my brother. My little coterie of fuckbuddies and hangers-on were going to steer clear of me and the media attention I dragged behind me. My relationship with Deacon was in a sick holding pattern. Amanda was still dead. I'd broken, or at least fractured, a lifelong bond of trust between me and my sisters and brother.

A little community service would go a long way to distracting me.

Bored, yet jumpy and upset, I went into the cafeteria. Dinner was starting. The staff placed trays of deluxe meals into the steam trays. I'd never see them again, those chattering people in hair nets, and I hadn't even gotten to know their names. I said good-bye in my mind to the cafeteria, the patio, the holes in the camera matrix. I said so long to the grey painted over everything, the flat lighting, the sterile corners. Karen came in, all unkind angles and protruding bones. I excused myself from Margie, who waved me off, and stood next to Karen as she plopped her journal on the tray.

"Hey," I said. "I'm getting my recommendation in, like, twenty minutes, then I'm outtie."

"It was good to see you again," she said flatly.

"You should call me when you get home. I mean it."

"I don't think I can do an Ojai again." She poked through a basket of perfect yellow bananas as if unable to choose one, though they all looked the same to me.

"Yeah, me neither." I said it, but did I mean it?

Deacon had kept me away from the life for months, but I didn't know where he and I stood. He might be out of my world forever, and if that was the case, then what did I have left but more of what had gone before? I found I wasn't looking forward to anything. I was terrified of speaking to Deacon, of being in my big empty condo. I didn't care to see Earl or Charlie. Didn't want to delve into what had happened with

Martin or Debbie. But mostly, I wasn't looking
forward to partying. Didn't want coke, but knew I'd
snort it when I got bored. Didn't want sex, but knew
I'd need it when I got sad.

Karen got to the bottom of the basket. The banana
at the end was black and soft. No one would want it.
She picked it up and put it on her tray instead of all the
firm, ripe ones.

I'd figure it all out once I was home. I might figure
it out licking the base of some guy's cock or tied to the
ceiling like an enraptured side of flesh, but I'd figure it
out. I just had to go deeper. Harder. Full throttle into
whatever tornado I'd walked into. Yet when I spoke,
something completely different came out.

"Something has to change," I said. "I don't think I
can live like that anymore."

"Yeah," Karen said pensively. "If I knew how to
stop doing this, I would."

"It's a problem. Me, I mean. I have a problem." I
said it with a little laugh, as if to disavow it even as I
said it. I was taking a practice run at thinking I had
something to fix. It was like an audition for recovery to
see if I had the talent to pull off the role.

"Fiona," Margie said, putting her hand on my
shoulder. "We're up."

I hugged Karen. "Good-bye. Eat something, would
you? You're skin and bones."

"I will. Good luck out there."

Elliot and Frances entered through the glass doors,
and I noticed that he was frowning. We walked in
silence to the conference room. I said good-bye to the

linoleum, the garden outside the window. Silently, as a prayer to people not present, I said good-bye to Jack who was completely unfuckable, Warren who was an act of violence waiting to happen, Mark who was one of a hundred or more.

I didn't know what waited for me outside. I didn't know if Deacon would take me back, didn't know if the media would crush me, but I was ready to be out of Westonwood—that was for damn sure.

CHAPTER 17

Mom didn't come back. It was just me and Margie with Elliot and Frances. The table shined in all its lacquer glory under the horizontal shadows of the window blinds. A black spider of a conference call unit sat in the middle of the table, ignored. I tried to make eye contact with Elliot, and he met my eyes once we sat. I saw no reassurances in the gaze, but he was never one to let a crack in his professional veneer show.

I tucked my hair behind my ears. Had I brushed it? I was about to go back into the world, and I'd hate to do it ungroomed, sloppy, with scraggly red hair and no makeup. I already felt as though I had one foot out the door.

"Ms. Drazen," Frances said to Margie, "can we get you anything?"

"Out of here?"

She smiled so disarmingly, Frances laughed, and the tension of the room broke a little.

"Well, thanks for coming." Frances looked as if she'd applied lipstick fifteen seconds before opening the glass doors. "This conversation is being recorded for the patient's protection."

I almost laughed out loud but choked it down.

Frances continued. "Doctor Chapman and I will be issuing our recommendations to the judge and district attorney for the City of Los Angeles, in the case of Fiona Maura Drazen." Frances folded her hands in front of her and looked me in the eye. "After careful consideration by the administration of this hospital, and the bearing in mind the counsel of Dr. Chapman, we've decided to recommend you stay at Westonwood or another accredited facility for an additional fourteen to forty-five days of observation, pursuant to Section 5250 of the California Welfare and Institutions code."

I swallowed. "Excuse me?"

"What's this about?" Margie demanded. "She's functioning. She's capable. I've seen far sicker people released on their own recognizance."

"She's had three violent outbursts while under our care," Frances said.

I spun on Elliot. "You said the meds caused the outbursts."

"I said maybe," he said gently. "I'm sorry, but—"

Frances broke in, "And she still has no recall of the incident."

"There was no incident," Margie growled. "You can ask Deacon Bruce."

"The judge thinks there was," Frances said. "He's concerned about letting a woman with psychotic episodes back into society."

"We just accepted a plea deal."

"From the prosecutor. Judge trumps lawyer."

Margie was holding herself together admirably, but I could see her gears turning. I bet the two psychologists across the table could as well.

"Our recommendation is that she be kept here for her own safety," Elliot said softly. He closed his little folder and stood. "I'm in session in two minutes. Excuse me." He nodded to each of us and strode out.

I was left sitting in shock. What had just happened?

I had been so sure I was leaving. I'd said good-bye to the place, checked my room for personal items, looked at the cafeteria for the last time. Staying was worse than a defeat. It was a humiliation.

How was I letting that motherfucker walk out of there?

I spun out of my chair and dashed into the reception area. He was just beyond the glass doors.

"Elliot," I called.

He slowed down, as if deciding what to do.

I ran to catch up. "What happened? Come on, you know I'm not going to hurt anyone."

He shook his head. "It's for the best."

"I'll have you in session tomorrow, and I'm not saying a word until you tell me what happened."

"Fiona, I—"

"You can shove your little pen tip up your ass. I'm going to make your life miserable."

He smiled ruefully and looked at the floor. "I'm not your therapist anymore. I'm going back to Compton."

"Fuck you are."

"I'm sorry I can't be here. I think you'll be just fine. You're doing great."

"Save the platitudes for the ones who need them."

His neck tensed, and his eyes got hard. That was my gotcha moment, and I didn't want it. His voice went from heavy cream to wire brush, and the stroke of every syllable drew blood. "Once you get out there with your cute little plea deal, you'll get eaten alive. Maybe by the press. Maybe by that man you almost killed. Maybe he'll kill you this time instead of breaking your teeth. The judge on your case is not out to help you, trust me. You don't have the tools to handle life outside these doors. You'll go back to using, and I'm not willing to wonder if I could have done something else to help you. I'm just going to do it. This is the only way to protect you."

"It was your job to assess my sanity. Not protect me."

He held his hands out, his clipboard clutched in his fingers. "That's just tough, Fiona. This was the last real thing I did here, and I'm okay with it."

"Fuck you."

He nodded, making me feel like a tantrum-prone child. And now what? He was going to say good-bye and leave me? No. Not allowed.

"This is not done," I said.

"Good-bye, Fiona. Meeting you was something else."

I turned around and ran back down the hall before he could say a word. I didn't know what I was trying to stop. Some freight train of my thwarted expectations before it ran me over? Maybe the moment where I would wake up and realize I'd failed, and I was stuck here? So help me God, I couldn't be there, cut off from everything for another month. Something had to be done, and if no one would do it for me, I would do it myself. I slammed past the glass doors, out of breath.

Margie stood staring at her phone.

"You have to keep Doctor Chapman here," I said in a breath. "Make them. He can't walk away."

Margie heard me, I knew she did. I was right there, but she wasn't listening.

"I fucked up," she said.

"How? You made a deal, they can't—"

"Dad was right. I'm too inexperienced. I would have had my finger on the judge's pulse if I'd known better."

What she was saying hit me like a slap.

"No," I said.

"I'm sorry, Fiona. I tried, but you need a better lawyer. It's not fair to you."

"Not fair to me? I'm here now with nothing and no one… I don't have Elliot, and now you're leaving? What am I supposed to do? Margie, how am I supposed to make it? Don't leave me." My hands were flying. I was screaming.

Margie was trying to grab my hands and shush me at the same time. "Calm down."

"Stay, and I'll calm down. Stay with me."

"I can't. It's not the best—"

"Don't leave me! Don't leave me! Don't leave me!"

When I tried to hold her close, hands on me pulled and tugged. There was a floor under me, and shadows in the light, and voices in all kinds of timbres and shades of gentleness. There was a discomfort in my arm like a stiff finger pushing against me, and soon after that, the hands relaxed, and everything went grey.

To be continued...

kick.

I've added a few chapters of book 2 – USE.
I hope you enjoy them.

kick.

CHAPTER 1.

FIONA

I often drifted off into a trance-like state that reminded me of the hypnosis sessions I used to have with Elliot. I fazed out in the evenings between dinner and lights out while I sat in front of the TV, watching the ocean waves on a loop, and I let my mind do whatever it wanted.

While I thought about nothing, in a cotton-candy medicated haze, the cardboard cone of my rage was hidden under the pink tufts of sugar. In the ten days since Elliot left, they'd changed my meds and I'd run the gamut from zoned out to acting out.

Too much slap, not enough tickle.

I missed Elliot and his cold professionalism, the little tics and movements he used to funnel his emotions, the promise of his naked body under his clothes. He'd been gone twelve hours before I started entertaining vivid sexual fantasies about him. I didn't need him for anything. In the heat of our non-relationship, I didn't need him to set me free or call me sane, so I didn't have to block out the thoughts. Since I'd rediscovered the feel of my fingers on my body, I'd entertained thoughts of him at night once, twice, three times after lights out, falling into a sleepless daze with my hands cupped over my cunt.

My favorite fantasy was so chaste it set my clit on fire.

I'm in a coffee shop on Charleville, the one where I could get a buttercup, which was a drip coffee with butter. I'm alone which, in and of itself, is a fantasy. There are no cameras or paparazzi anywhere. I sit at a table on the sidewalk and open a book. The sun shines. The breeze is light in my hair, and the mug is made of red porcelain.

He stands over me with his paper cup, casting a shadow on my book. "Fiona?"

I look up, and I put him together as I remember him: light brown hair, green/blue/grey eyes, narrow brows, long neck, and a smile that, for once, is genuine, unburdened by self-reproach or professional courtesy.

"Elliot, hi."

"How are you?"

"Great. Do you have time to sit?"

He always sits. Sometimes he's on his way somewhere and decides to take the time out, and sometimes he has nothing to do. But he always sits. I imagine our conversation. I have to make his life up,

because I know so little about him. I tell him how well
I am. How I'm cured. How I don't do drugs anymore
and how sex is no longer a need. Sometimes I tell him
I haven't had sex since I was released, and sometimes I
tell him I have, just a couple of times.

When I claim chastity, that's when the fantasy is
most vibrant. That's when he walks me to my car and
his words of affection, of longing, of repressed desire
pulse between my legs. The kiss I imagine, with his
hands on my face and his dick pushing against me,
makes me so wet I have to rub it off in my mental ward
cot.

I imagine going down to Compton, to some rat-
infested shelter or run-down church, and seeing him.
Our hurt for each other is so strong that the magnetic
pull makes our will to remain professional and proper
impossible.

He says, "I always wanted you."

I replayed our short time together, looking for
moments when that might have been true. As the days
wore on, I imagined he has me on the bed. He takes
my ankles and spreads my legs so far, and looks at my
wet cunt for a second before kissing it. The look on his
face is one of bliss, as if he'd been starving and
imprisoned and I was a great meal of freedom. When
he fucked me, he did it like in the movies, with his face
close to mine, eyes half closed, breathing my name.

I knew it was fantasy and impossible. I didn't
know the man at all, yet I did. He was normal, straight-
laced, probably vanilla. He'd never be with a fuck-up
sex addict, a druggie slave worthless whore camera-

magnet like me. I'd never attract a man who was plain nice. I didn't have access to the ordinary world, yet I craved it. My darkest desires were for an inaccessible normality.

I hadn't wanted that until Elliot left. In the days following, as my fantasies became more outrageously mild, I thought of Deacon, my master, the one who had helped me function and who I had betrayed. Maybe one day I'd remember the sticky web of circumstances that put us both in the stables, but did it matter a fuck? In the end, did I stab him to be free of him?

And free to do what?

Fuck? Snort? Party?

Or free to be normal?

CHAPTER 2.

ELLIOT

I didn't like rushing. If everything was done properly and in the right order, I never had to rush. Even the most tedious parts of the day could be managed effortlessly if they happened when they were supposed to.

On Tuesdays, I had therapy before work. As a therapist, I needed my own therapy sessions in order to maintain my sanity, though some weeks I had nothing to discuss and my sanity was only impaired by having to spend yet another fifty minutes in Lee's office, talking about nothing. Those sessions supposedly gave me an angle from which to see the seemingly unproductive sessions with my own patients, but I felt more and more like I was wasting my time.

I opened my car door. The bougainvillea that hung over the driveway needed a trim. I often did the trimming myself because I found it soothing, but since

I took the job at Westonwood, I had stopped. Since the gardeners had been instructed to leave it alone, they did, and it exploded into a waterfall of purple blooms that dropped onto my windshield.

I'd gone back to work at the Alondra Avenue Family Clinic in Compton. I'd left a chaplaincy there that had had a limited time frame. They'd asked me to stay on, but I went to Westonwood. When I left the enclave for the rich and troubled, I picked up some part-time work at Alondra while I sorted out my life. I didn't like the instability any more than I liked the upset schedule, but I needed the balance badly.

L.A. traffic was famously brutal, but it was easily managed if one took into consideration the season as it related to the LAUSD, the time of day, the weather, and were willing to change routes at a moment's notice. If I turned right on LaCienega at 7:01 a.m. on a normal Tuesday, I'd be on time. Turning at 7:02 made me upward of ten minutes late. I never figured out where the eight minutes went, but that extra sixty seconds seemed to increase the density of the traffic arteries by an order of magnitude.

So when I turned at 7:04, I assumed I'd have to apologize as soon as I walked into my session. That always led to an explanation of why I was late, and why it was important to be punctual, and back to how I felt about it, and so began the digging like kids in the yard, looking for treasure that wasn't there. But I'd forgotten that it was still Christmas break for the LAUSD, and the roads were clearish. I pulled into the alley behind Lee's office and took a deep breath. I'd made it, and I'd get to Alondra in time because the traffic was light. Being late for Lee was forgivable. Being late for my patients was egregious. They were people who had nothing reliable in their lives but me.

"Why do you worry about them?" asked Lee, her fingers laced together over her pregnant belly. She'd managed to get knocked up at forty-two, and I often found her in a state of bliss, sickness, or a meld of the two.

"Because I'm human. It's human to care."

"But it's not your job."

We'd had that discussion a hundred times. My job was to give patients a safe place to work on their problems. If I cared about them, I'd be emotionally shredded at the end of the week/month/year, and unable to work with the rest.

I didn't answer her. There was no point. I felt fidgety and caught myself rubbing my upper lip with my middle finger. I had nowhere to put the energy. I'd been that way since I left Westonwood.

"You were almost late this morning. I saw you pull in." Lee indicated the window beside her desk, looking onto the parking spaces. She didn't have any tics. World's perfect therapist, recommended by my mentor for her completely calm, organized, non-distracting demeanor.

"Jana caught me in the shower," I said, remembering the perfectly pleasant, if ill-timed lovemaking in the bathroom. "Set my morning back." She'd moved in six months before, after a whirlwind of dating, and had made little or no impression on the house except to be the prettiest thing that had ever stepped foot in the kitchen.

"Ah," she said. "Can I assume things are going well?"

"The usual. She wants me somewhere safe. She thinks I'm going to get jacked every day. She puts on a show of panic and worry. I soothe her. It works for a little while, et cetera et cetera…"

"And she wants you back at Westonwood."

"Yes."

"Did you tell her why you left?"

That was sticky, very sticky. Only Lee was qualified to unravel it, and she was the only person I'd trust with that level of complexity. I'd downloaded my desire to protect Fiona from her family and the media to her during the fist session after I left Westonwood, and she'd let me dance around it, waiting for me to describe my exact feelings in my own time.

"Jana wouldn't understand," I said.

"You should try."

"She's a delicate person. If I tell her about a patient's family pressuring me, she'll worry. If I tell her about the countertransference, it's worse."

"Countertransference happens. The thing with the girl's family, that's something she deserves to know, and it's well outside the privilege of the room."

"There's nothing to tell," I said. "That's what I told you—it was all inference. If I express inference, she's not going to have a place to put it, so it goes in the panic bucket. She can't deal with things that aren't facts."

"How are you going to live like that, Elliot?"

"You make my eyeballs ache, you know that?"

"You've said the same about Jana."

I sneered, knowing it was a sneer and she'd think it was funny. She was pointing out my transference, the redirection of feelings related to someone outside the room to the therapist. Transference was necessary. Countertransference, where the therapist placed unresolved feelings onto the patient, was trickier. Though it was normal, my countertransference with Fiona had to be dealt with. That was why we needed therapy for the therapy, to keep things in check.

"I didn't trust her father's motives," I said. "He comes in and tells me I should let her go. Tells me they'll take her in and watch her and thanks me very much for my time. The way he said it, it was off."

"So you think he should have asked you to keep her for more observation?"

"I think the fact that he even asked is a problem. If he'd asked me to feed her at noon, I would have fed her at eleven because I don't trust him."

"That's very reactionary," Lee said.

"You've never met the guy."

"And do you consider your decision meddling?"

"Anyone with a television knows what's going on. The media frenzy around her brother's accident and her stabbing her boyfriend; no sane person could survive it. She'd go back to using. Letting her out would have been setting her up for failure."

She leaned back in her chair. I didn't know if she needed the belly space or if she was taken aback by my tone.

"You believe that you made this decision based solely on the data?" she asked.

"Lee, what's the difference if it was the right decision?"

"You tell me."

I didn't, because I wasn't ready to say out loud that I had feelings for Fiona Drazen.

CHAPTER 3.

FIONA

I didn't require black dark to sleep, which was good since I fucked anywhere, any time, and sometimes I needed to drop off afterward. Once I woke up on top of Owen Branch on the floor of Club Permission Granted at ten thirty in the morning. All the lights were on, and ladies in blue smocks were vacuuming to the Spanish music on the boombox. Owen wasn't even fully awake when he lit a doob and handed it to me. I went back to sleep for another half an hour.

But at Westonwood, I had a problem I'd never had before: Everything kept me up. I knew I couldn't blame it on the light coming through the door window, or the crickets, or the whooshing of the pipes whenever someone, somewhere flushed.

It was stabbing Deacon and the waterfall of guilt that followed. Everything I'd done in my young life. Everyone heartbreak. Every careless betrayal. Every time I hurt someone to fulfill some minor need or wisp of a desire. For ditching Owen the morning after the high school prom. For sucking his dick the next week because it happened to be there. For throwing his phone out my car window on the 101 when he told me he'd snuck a shot of my mouth on his cock because it was such a pretty sight. For pulling the car over and punching him in the face, then telling everyone what he'd done until no one would hang out with him any more.

People in my position—meaning people other people looked at—didn't like Sneaky Petes taping fuck sessions, even if they told me nicely what they did and only did it for themselves. No. Just no. That was why phones were surrendered at Deacon's place.

But still. I wasn't focused on my rightness. My rightness didn't hurt, and I was after full-bore self-immolation. So I did what I did every night at Westonwood: I chose a random incident from my life and turned it over in the dark. That night it was Owen. I didn't have to punch him in the face. He'd been a harmless surfer with a huge dick and a permanent boner. I didn't have to make sure none of my friends spoke to him again, or throw his phone out the window on the freeway. It was expensive to him, and I hadn't given a fuck.

Somewhere, a toilet flushed. The pipes whooshed. It was morning.

***

I didn't tell my new therapist shit. She was just a bitch behind a desk who pretended to support my "healing process." The fact that I'd never put my fist in her face was a testament to my healing process, but I walked out of there twisted in knots every time. I was sure she and the fistful of drugs they gave me were the source of my insomnia. I hadn't slept more than a couple of hours a night since Elliot left.

"You're not schizophrenic," my new doctor bitch said. "You don't suffer from narcissistic personality disorder. You have no history of compulsion."

Her office was a museum of Native American artifacts. Dream-catchers. Masks. Beaded wall hangings and handmade blankets in frames.

"You're saying there's nothing wrong with me." I wasn't even hopeful, just killing time. We'd had that conversation a hundred times already. I didn't know what she was waiting for me to realize, because I'd have the epiphany of the century if I knew.

"The whole idea of sex addiction is a way to impose cultural models to make normal people seem abnormal. Mostly, these normal people are women. If you're not upset with your behavior, then there's nothing to say what you're doing is wrong."

"Then you're going to let me go?"

"What I'm trying not to do it pathologize your sexuality, but your mind is still not clear. Your memory is garbled, and I suspect you went through more in those stables than you're ready to admit. You're still prone to violence, mostly when men are in the room. I'd like to get to the bottom of it."

Considering I usually lost my shit in the cafeteria at about three o'clock, she was right. It was a co-ed facility, so there were always men around. The only time men weren't around was in that room with her.

"Do I need to be here for you to do that?" I asked. "Because you know, we're supposed get me back to functioning in society. This isn't a whole thing where I'm walking out some healed person who can get a job and land a good husband, right?"

"You're here. This time is for you. Think about it. I could buy you enough time to really get to the bottom of your issues with Deacon and your father."

She presented it like a birthday cake. The luxury of the century. An indefinite amount of time at Westonwood Spa, with the mental equivalent of hot rocks and exfoliating rubs, with her inferences about my father, who I hadn't mentioned to her, and Deacon, who was none of her business.

"And you walk out with what?" I said.

"I don't understand your meaning." She tilted her head, her pin-straight Brazilian blowout falling perpendicular to the earth while her face rested at the angle of inquisitiveness.

"I mean, we find some deep trauma in like, what two, three months, and you? It's a lot of work for you."

"It's work I love. Helping you to heal yourself," she said.

"Don't you have some high-paying gig in Beverly Hills?"

"I have a private practice, yes. Where are you going with this, Fiona? Are you afraid I'll abandon you like your last therapist?"

She should have known better. I'd cut her off the last time she'd tried to come down on Elliot for leaving, because I figured out that when he'd admitted to leaving to protect me, he'd only admitted it to me. I wouldn't betray him, and more than that, I respected him. But there she was, with her patronizing little smile and her forearms on the desk, accusing Elliot of shit outside her sphere of fucking knowledge.

I hated her. Maybe I hated her because she wasn't Elliot. Or maybe I hated her because I didn't want to be there. Maybe I just hated her because she was hateful, and because she was trying to get me to hate men instead of her Brazilian blowout.

And fuck, I hated her Brazilian blowout.

Most of our sessions went like that. I just disagreed with whatever she said. She said the sky was up, and I insisted I walked on clouds. She told me I was sick, and I said I was fine. She'd tried to con me into agreeing that my father had molested me, that Deacon beat me in a way that was non-consensual, that in fucking whomever I wanted, I'd agreed to be degraded. She couldn't get that the fucking itself wasn't degrading. The intentional degradation was degrading. And hot.

I didn't understand her. Why did she seem to care so much? Why couldn't she just listen to my problems, decide whether or not I was sane enough to be questioned, keep my meds low so I didn't feel like throwing things, and let me go? Surely the hospital didn't need my family's money that badly.

"It's not about money," Karen said one day at lunch. She was on a feeding tube and rolled her IV around with her. Mostly she was too weak to even get up, but when she did, she managed to find me. "You're like this rare creature. Rich. Famous. Living in a fish bowl. How many of you are there in the world? And you're in their chair. They can latch on to you and use you."

"For what? It's all confidential, isn't it?"

"Sure. But you know, over drinks? Who knows what they say at parties to get another client. Or to their own therapists. There aren't any secrets. My last guy wrote a paper about anorexia and wealth, and there was a patient in the paper who sounded just like me. My lawyer couldn't do anything."

"Jesus."

"Yeah. I don't tell these fuckers anything anymore. I don't tell anyone anything. Not even my friends."

What had I told Elliot? Anything? Everything? Dr. Brazilian Blowout hadn't gotten much more than evasion, but Elliot had gotten more from me before he split. I trusted him, but should I? I missed my fish-bowl friends who understood what to say when. I trusted them because they lived a shade of my life.

"It's not all like Ojai," I said. "You've been hanging out with the wrong people. Chill with me when you're out. We'll lay back. It's all on the DL."

"Really?"

"Yes." I pushed my food around. What if Elliot told everyone about me? That I was a sex-addict celebutante who didn't know how or why she'd stabbed the only man who loved her?

I didn't care what people thought, but imagining Elliot at a party, casually talking about my problems without mentioning my name, people's eyes going wide as they judged me—the scene I created bothered me. Elliot casually discussing my problems hurt in a way I couldn't even pin down. It was *him,* how *he* felt.

Did he feel nothing?

Was I just a curiosity to him?

Did he leave because he couldn't stand me?

I couldn't tolerate the thought, and I couldn't banish it from my mind. It played on a loop, and with each successive telling, he was more and more dismissive and contemptuous. I gripped my fork so tightly, the edge indented the flesh of my fingers. I pulled it away and looked at the brown-and-purple ridge it created. I ran my thumb over the skin. It was both numb and oversensitive.

"Did you sleep last night?" Karen whispered.

"No. I can't."

"Are they giving you something for it?"

"It's not working. I need Halcion. That's the only one that works."

When someone put their hand on my shoulder, I jumped.

"Sorry," Frances said. "I didn't mean to frighten you."

I hadn't heard her come up behind me. "It's okay."
I said it, but I didn't mean it. She dealt with people like
me all day. She knew how to approach. But I was so
tired I was docile.

"You have visitors."

I didn't know why I thought it might be Deacon. I
still held some childish hope that he'd come get me.
The thrill of the thought must have been all over my
face.

"It's your sisters."

CHAPTER 4.

FIONA

My sisters.

I had six of them, and a brother. So though Frances had said it as if she was talking about a complete set, there was no way all of them had shown up at Westonwood all at once.

Margie got up as I walked out onto the patio, and she hugged me.

"I'm sorry, sweetheart," she said. "I'm sorry I left you." She pushed me away, holding my biceps. "You look good."

"Are you my lawyer again?"

"No. I just came to see you."

"I didn't like that other guy."

"He's very experienced," Theresa said from behind Margie. "He already got you a new judge."

"Jesus, Theresa. Don't sneak up on me like that." I hugged her, and when we separated, she got her hair back into place.

Some girls become stuck-up bitches early in life, and at eighteen, Theresa was just as stuck up as any of them. Always good, always correct. She sat up straight and chewed with her mouth closed, said please and thank you and dressed right for the occasion. It was an accident of her birth, that perfection. None of the rest of us were as pin straight as she was. She wore her little soup of redheaded genes like a tiara. I had no idea why she even showed up to see me. She hated me.

"So?" I said, throwing myself onto the garden bench and spreading my legs in an unladylike fashion. I wanted to throw my whore body in her face, just to make her uncomfortable. "How are you guys?"

"I'm fine," Theresa replied, pressing her knees together. "How are you?"

"Crazy. What do you want?"

"I came checking after you. It's a courtesy."

"Great, I'm having tea with Spence and Chip at three, then a little badminton. Shall you join for a swipe at the shuttlecock?" I tipped my head back toward the field where the croquet and badminton had been set up.

"Oh, Fiona." Margie swung a chair around.

"Small talk is a lubricant, not an insult," Theresa huffed.

"I've never needed lubricant unless I'm getting it in the ass."

I'd aimed to shock her, and I'd done it. Her face, a mask of perfection under her red ponytail, seemed to fall for a second. I thought I'd hit home until she laughed. Then Margie laughed. I felt a swell of pride in pleasing them, even though Theresa was younger and hateful, and I was mad at Margie. It was as if, in that laugh, they accepted me. They didn't, I knew that, but it was my moment.

"Okay, guys. I'm busy finding wholeness," I said. "Seriously. Why didn't you come with Mom and Dad?"

"They're busy," Margie cut in.

"Yeah, more like, Mom hates discomfort, and since she came around here last time asking if Dad ever touched me, I'm thinking I'm not a happy sight for her right now."

"What did you tell her?" Margie's voice was clipped.

I pressed my lips together then puckered them. "He never touched me."

"Is that what you told her, or is that just a fact?" Margie asked.

"Both."

She scanned my face, looking for any other tidbit, like an open pledge I'd betrayed or the slip of an unsavory truth.

"What do you want from me, Margaret?"

"The judge changed. Dad wants you out. Why, is a matter of speculation," she said.

"He wants to divert attention," Theresa said softly, into her hands. "Away from what's happening with

Jonathan. I know him. I know how he thinks." She held up her hand, but she looked reluctant to open pledge. As second youngest, she rarely did. There was a tacit, unspoken courtesy to the elders that they opened it.

"I swear to god," I said, holding up my hand, "sixty percent of my brain capacity is taken up by what's said under pledge and who was under pledge when it was said. I'm not that bright, guys. Don't fill up the bucket, or it's gonna spill."

"Pledge open," Theresa said.

"Okay, go."

"Jonathan." All Margie said was our brother's name, and the beginning of that potentially long sentence ended in silence. The chatter of birds and insects in the garden seemed too loud to bear.

"I know there was something with his girlfriend…" Something about it nagged me, as if I'd met her or done something I should be ashamed of.

"Rachel. She's dead," Theresa said, closing her eyes as if gathering strength. Margie put her hand over Theresa's and let her finish. "Sheila had a party Christmas night. Rachel and I went two days before to help her set up. She knew the neighborhood. So, night of the party, Rachel shows after most of the family leaves. Jonathan gets drunk and starts acting like an ass. She takes off in his car and…." She cleared her throat before continuing. "They found the car, but not the body."

"I'm sorry," I said.

"Rachel was my friend. She had a tough home life, so she came back to the house with me a lot. Dad, he… Well, she started getting all gifts and wouldn't say from where, and this was a few years ago. So." She cleared her throat again, and her eyes darted over the garden.

"She and Dad, when she was fifteen," Margie cut in with her businesslike tone.

Theresa picked up the thread. "Jon didn't know until a few weeks ago."

"None of us did," Margie said.

"It's the creepiest thing ever," I said. "Seriously, I thought his thing with Mom was like true love that transcended age. I'm a rose-colored dumbfuck."

"You shouldn't use words like that."

"Fuck fuck fuck."

"Can you stop? This doesn't need to be harder." Theresa's face was tense, her fingers clenched into hooks.

Margie glanced at me, her look telling me to shut the fuck up. Delivering bad news was usually Margie's job, but Theresa seemed hell bent on saying hard things, and it appeared Margie was backing her up.

"Okay, go on," I said.

"They haven't told you because they didn't want to upset you."

"They don't want to upset themselves."

"Jon tried to commit suicide," Theresa said.

"What? When?"

"Little less than a week ago." Her voice dropped. "I found him. He took a handful of pills and gave himself a heart attack. It was awful. I mean, really awful. It's going to break Mom."

I looked at Margie. "He's okay?" My brother, the only boy and the youngest of eight, was the scion, the gem, and an arrogant ass I'd never want harmed.

"He's fine. They admitted him here last night. Supposedly Mom is coming this afternoon to tell you, but you know how that goes."

"Here? They admitted him *here*?"

Margie grabbed Theresa's hand, relieving her of the responsibility of speaking. "They don't send you home after a suicide attempt. They have to figure out if you're a risk to yourself. It's like babysitting, only really fucking expensive."

"You don't have to say that word," Theresa whispered. Theresa turned toward the patio.

In the direct light, I saw she had dark circles under her eyes, and renegade hairs had escaped her ponytail. She'd lost her friend, and her brother had almost died. She had a sister in an institution and a father who liked girls slightly younger than her. I realized she was as much of an addict as I was, and refinement was her drug of choice.

"Are you okay, Theresa? You look like hell," I said.

"She was my friend, but she was also a little in love with money, which is probably why she went from Dad to Jon… God, it's even hard to say that."

"Not easy to hear either."

"I think she was trying to blackmail Dad," Theresa said. "It's such a mess. I've never seen Dad like this. He's *afraid*. That's scarier than anything."

"He's not scared," Margie cut in. "He's playing at it. And yes, she was trying to blackmail Dad. I got that through my own channels."

"Why didn't he just pay it?"

"Maybe he did," Margie said. "But she kept coming after him."

"Then me," Theresa said. "She kept saying hateful things to me about Jonathan and Dad, like she was trying to get me to hate them. I was weird about her dating my brother, then I wasn't. Now I am again. But when you see Jonathan, can you tell him I'm sorry? We had this big fight just before. I called him names, which was… I don't know what came over me." Her hands sat palm up in her lap, and she stared at them. "We can't fight amongst ourselves. Reporters are asking questions. It's nuts out there. They're asking about Rachel, about you. They want to use us. Everyone has a camera, and I don't want us to be used any more."

"We're the world's circus," I said. "Third ring to the right. I don't know how to shake it."

"I'm going to." Theresa set her jaw, and a steel curtain dropped over her face. "I'm going to be normal. I'm going to work and have a job like anyone else. I'm going to have friends who like me for me. Not for money or fame or any of this."

"Good luck with that," I said, already shaking my head over her failure to achieve the dream of being no better than ordinary.

On the way out, with Theresa half a hall away, Margie took my hand. "Keep your shit together, and you can get out. Your mandated time is only a few more days, and your boyfriend's not pressing charges, so you can probably avoid a lot of questioning and ugliness if you stay low. But a little sisterly advice."

"As opposed to what you usually give?"

"Jonathan's going to need you. He's not himself. Be there for him. It really is a circus. They've been poking around Dad, which means there are going to be questions."

"I told Mom to talk to Carrie. I'm sorry, I just—"

"It's okay. Forget it."

"Carrie always knew Dad had a thing for... I can't even say it. I always thought she... I can't say that either." I couldn't say that Carrie had always maintained that Dad liked young girls, and that made me think she'd gotten some form of sexual attention none of the rest of us had. I had no proof, just a twist in the gut. Carrie had never said one way or the other.

"Carrie can take care of herself," Margie said. "If I were you, I'd stay in here as long as possible. As a matter of fact, I'd like to admit myself right now."

"If you were in here, I'd work like hell to get you out."

"You're implying... what?"

"You ditched me."

She put her hands on her hips. "For your own good."

"Isn't it about time other people stopped deciding what was for my own good? Maybe treat me like an adult who can make her own decisions? I have my own reason for wanting you to be my lawyer, and it has nothing to do with your experience. I don't want to explain myself to some strange, experienced person. I need someone to work with who I am. Do you get it?"

She didn't answer. She pecked me on the cheek and stalked off for the door. From Margie, that might as well have been a signature on the dotted line.

Thank you for reading. Book 2 is called Use, Book 3 is called Break. I hope you like Fiona's story. Thank you for indulging me on this difficult journey with a difficult girl.

If you fancy something complete (and borderline sane), you should try *The Submission Series*, the story of Jonathan Drazen, sixteen years after the incidents here. It's kinky and dirty, and Jonathan grows up to be a perfect book boyfriend. Get the bundles or check out Book One, *Beg*. It's free, and the series is complete.

Theresa Drazen's relationship with mafia capo Antonio Spinelli are documented in The Corruption Series: *Spin, Ruin*, and *Rule*, wherein all her attempts at lawfulness and peace fail in the name of love. This series is complete.

I'm on Goodreads, Facebook, Pinterest, Tumblr, Twitter and Instagram with varying degrees of frequency.

My email is cdreiss.writer@gmail.com.

You can sign up for the mailing list at cdreiss.com, which is the best way to find out what I'm up to.

I would greatly appreciate a review at the online retailer where you bought this book.

CPSIA information can be obtained
at www.ICGtesting.com
Printed in the USA
LVHW05s0436180718
584193LV00004B/330/P

9 781499 537536